"You'r...
she ...

"Perhaps," he conceded. A cool smile played on his lips and his eyes mocked her.

She tried to pull her wrist free but when he resisted she forced herself to relax and stared into his gray eyes. "This compulsory bedding you subject me to every couple of months or whenever the whim takes you has got to stop."

He said softly, "Compulsory?"

"Yes . . ." But, while she tried to say it firmly, she felt a cruel heat rising from the base of her throat, and she bit her lip.

LINDSAY ARMSTRONG married an accountant from New Zealand and settled down—if you can call it that—in Australia. A coast-to-coast camping trip later, they moved to a six-hundred-acre mixed-grain property, which they eventually abandoned to the mice and leeches and blackflies. Then, after a winning career at the track with an untried trotter, purchased "mainly because he had blue eyes," they opted for a more conventional family life with their five children in Brisbane, where Lindsay now writes.

Books by Lindsay Armstrong

HARLEQUIN PRESENTS
1183—HEAT OF THE MOMENT
1295—ONE MORE NIGHT
1327—A LOVE AFFAIR
1439—THE DIRECTOR'S WIFE
1487—LEAVE LOVE ALONE
1546—A DANGEROUS LOVER

HARLEQUIN ROMANCE
2582—PERHAPS LOVE
2653—DON'T CALL IT LOVE
2785—SOME SAY LOVE
2876—THE HEART OF THE MATTER
2893—WHEN THE NIGHT GROWS COLD
3013—THE MARRYING GAME

LINDSAY ARMSTRONG

Dark Captor

Harlequin Books

TORONTO • NEW YORK • LONDON
AMSTERDAM • PARIS • SYDNEY • HAMBURG
STOCKHOLM • ATHENS • TOKYO • MILAN
MADRID • WARSAW • BUDAPEST • AUCKLAND

Harlequin Presents first edition July 1993
ISBN 0-373-11569-5

Original hardcover edition published in 1991
by Mills & Boon Limited

DARK CAPTOR

CHAPTER ONE

STEPHANIE RAYBURN sat motionless on her stool and stared at her blank canvas with her chin in her hands.

She was in her early twenties, very slim and rather tall with pale skin, coppery hair she almost always wore tied or plaited back, and hazel eyes that sometimes looked green, sometimes gold.

Finally she blinked several times then sighed as it occurred to her that she was using a technique she rarely employed, the last in her range of techniques, in fact, before she admitted she was totally without inspiration. It worked on the principle that this pristine canvas had some mysterious secret which she had to draw from it as well as the depths of her mind. Some Elysian field perhaps, *something* that was meant to be painted on to it but not, obviously, the flowers, trees and shrubs that grew beyond the terrace where she sat, catching the morning sunlight so attractively and filling the air with their lovely woody and lemony scents yet not communicating themselves to her at all, sadly.

And if her last technique failed—she sighed again to think of it—there was only one thing to do: place herself beyond reach of canvas and oils, even paper and pencil, for some time. Yes, even when the craving to be painting starts to grow again you have to be strong, she told herself, and fight it for a while . . .

That was when she realised the phone in the study just inside the french doors from where she sat was ringing and she got to it just as her stepmother arrived looking faintly annoyed and out of breath—which meant it might have been ringing for a while.

Stephanie smiled at her apologetically. 'Sorry,' she murmured, 'I was miles away... Hello?'

'Mrs Rayburn? May I speak to Mrs Stephanie Rayburn, please?'

'Speaking...'

There was a pause then the voice on the other end, sounding strained and embarrassed, continued, 'Mrs Rayburn, this is Sally Retford. I'm Mr Rayburn's new secretary. He's asked me to let you know...' again a pause, palpably awkward '...he's asked me to let you know he'd like you to be at the Sheraton Hotel tomorrow and I've booked you a room for the night. It'll be available from eleven o'clock.' The last bit came out in a rush.

Stephanie went still and her stepmother, who was watching her, narrowed her eyes.

'Mrs Rayburn?'

'Yes...' Stephanie cleared her throat. 'Yes. Thank you, Sally.' She put the phone down and turned to stare out over the garden.

'Dominic?' Nan Williams hazarded as she eyed Stephanie's taut back beneath her paint-splashed overalls.

'Yes.'

'Stephanie——'

But Stephanie turned to her urgently. 'Don't. Please don't, Nan. We've said it all so many times but nothing can alter the fact that when he calls the tune I have to dance to it.'

Nan started to say something sharp but she bit her lip and said only, 'It's been a long time, this time. Two—three months?'

'Four.'

'How long will you be gone?'

'One night so far as I know, but *this* time...' It was Stephanie's turn to stop and bite her lip.

'Take the car,' Nan said gently.

'No, I'll take the bus, just in case,' her step-daughter replied bitterly and added with an effort, 'I'd worry about you stranded out here without a car.'

Nan stared at her then walked up to her and hugged her briefly. 'You're a good kid,' she said gruffly. 'I just wish... but there, I won't say it.'

'And I'll never forget all you've done for me, Nan, and what you did for Dad,' Stephanie said intensely.

It was those sentiments she tried to concentrate on as the bus bore her towards Brisbane and Dominic Rayburn the next morning, instead of the tension she could feel mounting within her.

She couldn't remember her mother, who had died leaving her and her twin brother to the dazed, grief-stricken mercy of their father, who was entering middle age and was, anyway, a vague scholarly man to whom small children were a race apart. How he'd coped in those early years Stephanie had never known. She did know that her childhood had not been carefree although she'd been extremely well-educated because of her father's insistence—he was a university lecturer in ancient history—on sending her and Mike to very expensive private schools, which had kept him relatively poor. She remembered the series of rented houses they'd lived in and how she'd gradually taken charge of their living so that by the time she was thirteen she was a good cook and housekeeper and spent a lot of her free time from school doing the washing and ironing. She also remembered how this role had set her apart from her peers at school not only because their lives were so different but because she had had a competence and maturity they had lacked—about some things. She doubted whether it had ever really dawned on her father that it might be a handicap to his children to be thrown in with the children of the rich and famous, but some of the memories still had the power to hurt her, she knew. And of course her twin brother, Mike, had brought that particular lesson home with a vengeance.

But I won't think of Mike, she told herself as the bus bore her even closer to Brisbane. I'll think instead of Dad and Nan meeting and marrying: two lonely people who found real love when they least expected it—if only they could have had longer together. And think of how Nan treats me like the daughter she never had and shares her house with me so I can paint in peace and keep her company at the same time—and hardly ever comments on Dominic and why he won't let me go...

As usual, her arrival at the hotel caused a bit of a stir—the name of Rayburn always did although Mrs Dominic Rayburn was not quite what people expected, and she caught the glint of surprise in the receptionist's eyes as she glanced at Stephanie's jeans and cotton jacket, her one small, battered overnight bag, her lack of make-up and her short, unpainted nails.

And as usual there were no messages but then there never were—that wasn't Dominic's style. He expected her to wait until he turned up, but as she looked around the luxurious room she'd been conducted to a spark of rebellion lit her eyes. I'm damned if I will, she thought. I'll go shopping, have some lunch and come back when it pleases me. And then I'll tell him he can go to hell this time because...

She broke off mid-thought and swung round tensely at the sound of a key in the door—it was too soon, she wasn't ready to face him yet, she needed more time... More time, she thought mockingly as the door swung open. You've had four months.

'Stephanie,' Dominic Rayburn said by way of greeting as he strolled into the room, and, as always, she was reminded of how, from the first time she'd laid eyes on him, her life had never been the same.

She closed her eyes briefly, commanding those memories to go away, then said quietly, 'Hello, Dominic.'

Their gazes clashed as he stopped in front of her, his steely grey and enigmatic, hers bitter and faintly wary.

Dominic Rayburn was thirty; he had thick straight dark hair, a tall, streamlined build, an aquiline nose and the kind of good looks that stopped women in their tracks. If that weren't enough, he also now had an air of arrogance, sophistication and success—perhaps it had always been there, she'd often thought, but nowadays there was no mistaking it even if you didn't *know* he could be a satanic enemy and hated him at times more than you'd thought it possible to hate. Yet times when...

'It's been a while,' he said, breaking into her thoughts.

'Yes. Four months.'

He raised an eyebrow. 'You've been counting?'

She shrugged.

He looked her over from head to toe, making her conscious of her simple attire, her hair, which was drawn back into one thick, heavy plait apart from some feathery strands that had escaped, and said with a trace of irony, 'Nothing's changed, I see, except that you've lost weight.'

Stephanie's mouth tightened. 'I was always thin,' she countered.

'Yes,' he agreed thoughtfully, 'except for where it mattered——'

'You don't have to flatter me, Dominic,' she broke in tautly. 'I've learnt to live with being like a beanpole.'

'My beautiful beanpole wife,' he murmured with a faint dry smile, 'who still has such a chip on her shoulder. You know as well as I do, Stephanie...' his eyes glinted '...that beneath that no-frills exterior you cultivate so assiduously is an exquisitely delicate and sensual body. May I take it since you've been counting the months that you've missed my attentions to it?'

Stephanie caught her breath and at the same time reined in her anger—she'd been down that road too often. 'No more than you've missed paying any attention to it,' she said coolly and went to turn away, but he caught her wrist.

'Ah, but I have,' he said softly. 'What other reason would I have for bringing you here? I enjoy the way you make love to me, Stephanie. I've told you that before——'

'You're a devil,' she breathed.

'Perhaps,' he conceded, 'but it's so interesting to see you doing battle with yourself, to see you hating me, hating yourself for wanting me and sometimes you put up a marvellous fight—I quite admire you for it—then to see you revelling in the things I do to you.' A cool smile played on his lips and his eyes mocked her.

'We obviously have different views of it,' Stephanie said grimly, thinking, If there's one thing I'll *never* do it's admit any of this. She tried to pull her wrist free but when he resisted she forced herself to relax and stared into his grey eyes. 'In fact,' she went on steadily although her heart was beating rapidly, 'that's something I wanted to tell you. This compulsory *bedding* you subject me to every couple of months or whenever the whim takes you has got to stop.'

He said softly, *'Compulsory?'*

'Yes . . .' But, while she tried to say it firmly, she felt a cruel heat rising from the base of her throat, and bit her lip. Then her shoulders sagged and she stared at him with something like despair in her eyes. 'What do you want me to do, Dominic? Go down on my knees and beg you to let me go? Is that what it's all about?'

He released her wrist abruptly. 'We could live together as man and wife,' he said harshly.

'You know that wouldn't work! I'm about as far removed as it's possible to be from the kind of wife you... If my brother hadn't embezzled money from you I wouldn't even *be* your *wife*.'

'And if I hadn't been your first lover——'

'Only lo——' She stopped.

They stared at each other until he said, 'Is that so? All the more reason, then, as your first and only lover...' he managed to inject a withering scepticism into his voice '...to have this curiosity about you, Stephanie——'

'You know you were the first,' she said thoughtlessly, then winced.

'I'm not disputing that.' He shrugged. 'And if all you say is true then I also feel I have a responsibility towards you, my dear. I really do.'

She swallowed because anger and something else were making it difficult for her to speak. 'It's not that at all, Dominic. It's revenge. Because all those years ago you thought you'd made a conquest, unwittingly, perhaps, but all the same, and you were prepared to grant me a little while, a few weeks with you while I was a novelty, before you dropped me. But I wasn't looking for charity.'

'What were you looking for, as a matter of interest?' he queried sardonically.

She blushed again but murmured, 'Not to feel like a poor relation or a freak at a side-show, probably.'

'That still rankles,' he said meditatively, 'although you denied it at the time. May I point out yet again that it was my sister Melissa who uttered those thoughtless words?'

'Your sister Melissa has one good trait,' Stephanie said bleakly. 'She is an utter snob but completely honest about it.'

Dominic looked amused. 'I agree with you.'

Stephanie took a breath. 'Then we might agree about something else,' she said quietly. 'It's over a year since you took me hostage——'

'Is that what I did?'

'Yes, you did,' Stephanie continued even more quietly but her gaze was contemptuous, 'for two reasons. Because I dented your pride once and because you needed my brother even though he was a thief and stole from you—to put it in its harshest terms.'

'He did steal from me.'

Stephanie stared at him and the incredible irony of it all swept over her yet again. Of course he was right. Her brilliant but erratic twin had misappropriated a substantial sum of money and the fact that he'd bet it on a horse and had intended to return it before anyone was aware of the loss, as well as enrich himself in the process, only made it less than stealing in *his* eyes. Of course the horse hadn't won—that was Mike's kind of luck—and he'd come to her desperate and distraught and staring in the face not only the wrecking of his career as a boat designer—but also prosecution for theft. But then the irony went way back. Dominic Rayburn had inherited the family shipyard on the Brisbane River—why had it to be his shipyard where Mike had the job he'd dreamed about from childhood? And why, when Mike had begged her to go and see Dominic Rayburn because she and Melissa Rayburn had been classmates all their school lives, had she given in and been unable to tell her brother that the last man on earth she felt able to confront in any circumstances was Melissa's tall, dynamic brother?

Because for all his faults you couldn't stand by and watch Mike go to goal, she reminded herself. So you went with the proposition that you would underwrite the debt and make sure that every last cent was paid off with interest although it would take time... That was when Dominic had made his incredible counter offer: marry me and I won't proceed with any charges, I'll even let Mike stay on and pay the money back gradually out of his wages; he certainly has some brilliant ideas and perhaps this will teach him a lesson—that's the only bargain I'm prepared to make...

'All right, he stole from you,' she said bleakly, coming back to the present. 'And you were right; I think he got such a fright and was so grateful for the chance to redeem himself that he does seem to have reformed. But, for the record, I still don't understand why you had to make this particular bargain.' She fiddled with the plain gold wedding band on her left hand.

'I'm not a philanthropic institution,' he observed. 'Although I did think it was quite a generous offer actually, considering your alternative, which consisted of putting your painting on hold and going back to the town planners office to work your guts out to pay the money back. But it also suited me to get married, Stephanie, and it certainly suited me to bring you down a peg or two,' he said quite pleasantly. 'But I've told you all this before.'

'You've never told me *why* it suited you to get married,' she said jerkily.

He studied her. 'If you really want to know, I'll tell you now,' he said at last and his lips twisted, 'although you may like it even less. When I took over Rayburn's from my father, which was not long before you came back into my life, the company was in a bad way—something that wasn't generally known, but I urgently needed capital or it could have gone under. As it happened, my grandmother had bequeathed me rather a lot of money but she was an eccentric old lady and, whether from malice aforethought or because she did have my best interest at heart, she stipulated in her will that I could not inherit it until I had entered the state of matrimony.'

Stephanie's lips parted incredulously.

'Don't look so stunned, my dear,' he said mildly. 'It's not often that one is able to combine business with pleasure as successfully as we have been able to.'

'I hate you,' Stephanie said conversationally. 'You have to be the most cold-blooded, cynical...'

'Bastard?' he supplied. 'It's odd you should say that. I had you figured for the feminine version of those attributes.' There was undoubted mockery in his eyes.

'And now——' She broke off and looked away.

'Do you know, I still don't know what to make of you? But I will say this, you're the strangest mixture of consistency and vulnerability.'

Their gazes caught and held and she knew exactly what he meant, and winced.

His eyes narrowed but he went on in the same even, dispassionate tones, 'But do continue. You were going to lecture me on this compulsory bedding I subject you to, I take it?'

'Don't tell me it isn't what you have in mind for tonight,' she said bitterly. 'Your quarterly collecting of the dues—and while we're on the subject...' her eyes flashed suddenly ' ... I'm sure you have no compunction about embarrassing *me* but your new secretary was extremely embarrassed yesterday and, if you must know, it incenses me to be humiliated like that! You could at least ring me yourself.'

'Dear Stephanie...' his eyes glinted '...when you stormed off after our brief—er—honeymoon and made it abundantly clear you wouldn't live with me or accept any support from me and only sleep with me under duress, you're lucky I didn't sack your brother there and then, and then sue him for the debt he owed me. So I should ignore the odd pinprick if I were you. But actually...' he paused '...I have something different in mind this time.'

'I'm all agog,' she said deliberately.

He smiled. 'I want you to come away with me for a few days, and I want you to play the part of a loving wife. Think you could manage that?' He raised his eyebrows at her.

'No,' Stephanie said baldly.

'Not even if I were to say that, providing you play your part well enough, I'll consider ending our marriage?'

Her eyes widened and she sat down on the end of the bed suddenly. 'Do...' She swallowed. 'Do you really mean that?'

The expression in his eyes was enigmatic. 'I generally mean what I say.'

'Where...and why?' she stammered.

He said coolly, 'Why need not concern you. As for where—Hayman Island.'

Stephanie blinked several times.

'So?'

'Well...' she took an uncertain breath '...I'd not have the right clothes. Isn't it supposed to be the best of the Whitsunday resorts?'

He shrugged. 'Clothes can be easily rectified and if you're about to parade your famous inferiority complexes before me...' he looked at her ironically '...isn't it about time you grew out of all that, Stephanie?'

She bit her lip and stared at her hands.

'After all,' he went on softly, 'you could be joining the ranks of the rich and famous yourself soon. Your last exhibition, to which you did not invite me, was quite successful from what I hear.'

Stephanie gripped her hands in her lap and wondered if he knew that the one serious inferiority complex she now had was inextricably linked to him.

She shivered inwardly and looked up at last. 'All right, if we have a bargain.'

Their gazes locked.

'Excepting that I might not be much good in the role of a loving wife,' she said a little helplessly.

'I might be able to help there.' A glimmer of amusement lit his eyes.

'But I still haven't got the right clothes—when would we go?'

'Tomorrow. I didn't think clothes mattered to you,' he observed.

'Tomorrow!' She gestured with her hands.

'They do?'

'Well I can't go to Hayman Island in what I've got with me,' she said defensively.

'You could go out and shop this afternoon,' he countered.

Stephanie stared at him, her mind in turmoil as she realised she wouldn't know where to begin because the truth was clothes didn't mean much to her now and hadn't since...

'Or I could get in an expert,' he said.

She frowned confusedly.

'I know someone who...' he shrugged '...has a fashion consultancy. She'd know what you'd need, where to get it, and she could bring it all here for your approval. She'd probably have to check you out first for size and style.'

'Style,' Stephanie said with a dry little laugh then she sighed and rubbed her face. 'You'd better get her in, then. You are—you are serious, though, aren't you?' She searched his eyes warily.

'I've told you,' he replied.

'And there'll be no consequences for Mike when we end it?'

'Provided he keeps on the straight and narrow.'

'Is there someone else?' What made her say it she didn't know, and she coloured faintly and turned away from him to hide it.

'Would you care, Stephanie?' His words were quiet—and deadly, she thought, because, God help her, she doubted if she would ever rid herself of Dominic Rayburn.

'No,' she said equally quietly, turning her head and looking up at him. 'No.'

CHAPTER TWO

'How do you do, Stephanie?' A pair of sparkling dark eyes roved over Stephanie's person then their owner turned to Dominic Rayburn, saying, 'My dear Dominic, you didn't tell me!'

'Tell you what, Marie?'

'That your charming wife has the figure of a top model as well as unusual beauty. It will be a pleasure to dress her, an absolute pleasure!'

Dominic Rayburn grinned at his 'expert', Marie Baldwin, who was in her early forties yet looked like a model herself. 'Must have slipped my mind,' he drawled, and added, 'Then I can leave you to it?'

'Assuredly,' Marie said briskly, her accent leaving no doubt she was French despite her surname.

'Fine, I'll be back this evening. Just charge it all to me.'

'I love the sound of that,' Marie said with a twinkle as the door closed behind him. 'And I don't know why I should be surprised about you—less than the best would never do for Dominic. It's just that...' her brow creased '...to be honest I didn't even know he was married.'

'We...' Stephanie hesitated, still showing her surprise, and started again. 'I'm a painter and not very social, which is why I need your help,' she said wryly.

Marie studied her unabashedly. 'So we should start from scratch?' she said slowly, her dark eyes thoughtful.

'Well, yes, if you wouldn't mind,' Stephanie said awkwardly, thinking of her Woolworths' underclothes. 'But one thing—I hate fussy, complicated clothes and I'm not very good at wearing them.' She grimaced.

Marie continued to study her, saying, 'You are honest—I appreciate that in a client. And you are right; simplicity will become you best although with your figure you could wear anything and get away with it. But it's a question of one's aura, is it not? And yours is rather different. Don't worry—I won't make you into a copy of every other socialite about. What about make-up? Do you never wear it?'

'Hardly ever.'

Marie's eyes twinkled again. 'I think you could wear some without compromising yourself, you know. Here's a thought—while I'm whizzing about chasing up a wardrobe for you, why don't I send someone over to show you how it can be done v-e-r-y discreetly?'

Stephanie considered then thought, Why not go the whole hog? Besides, she couldn't help liking Marie. 'Yes. And if my hair needs anything——'

'No,' Marie said definitely. 'It's . . . you. But I'll find you some beautiful scarves to tie it back as a change from the plait.'

'I'm relieved something can stay the same,' Stephanie said ruefully, causing Marie to narrow her eyes—but she forebore to comment. And after making some quick notes about sizes she left with a cheerful *au revoir*.

It was nine o'clock that evening when Stephanie rang room service and ordered a snack and coffee, which she and Marie tucked into with gusto.

'So, you are happy?' Marie enquired.

Stephanie grinned at her. 'I feel like a new woman from the skin out.'

'But—your own woman?'

Stephanie gazed around, at the pile of exquisite underwear on the bed, at the beautiful soft, subtle colours of the garments that were draped across the backs of chairs, the shoes, the two new pieces of leather luggage, the cosmetics, then back at Marie. 'Yes,' she said quietly. 'Thank you. That was rather understanding of you.'

Marie shrugged, a very Gallic movement. 'It is my art as yours is yours. Just remember, wear them with confidence because I can assure you you're entitled to. I hope Dominic will be happy too and not think I've spent too much of his money,' she added ruefully.

'I'm sure that won't be a problem,' Stephanie said coolly.

Marie stared at her, an oddly narrow little glance, then turned away and Stephanie felt the colour stealing into her cheeks. And, perhaps because this woman had understood things about her that others didn't, she heard herself saying, to her surprise, 'This—as you might have guessed—is not a very normal marriage.' She opened her hands. 'And——'

'You don't have to explain,' Marie broke in swiftly.

Stephanie winced. 'It wasn't that I felt I had to. Nor is it a state secret I'm giving away——'

'It wasn't what I meant either—that I was uninterested or it was distasteful,' Marie broke in again, equally swiftly. 'Marriages of convenience are much better understood where I come from, I think. Do you love him?' she asked directly.

Stephanie looked away. 'No,' she said huskily and added to herself, 'How could I?'

But Marie heard and she said drily, 'Sometimes that does not enter into it at all. Have you ever considered giving him a run for his money?'

Stephanie smiled slightly. 'No. But anyway, there'd be no point.'

'Ah,' Marie said wisely, 'but who ever knows that? Why does he stay married to you, I wonder? Dominic Rayburn could have anyone he chose, one feels.'

Stephanie sighed. 'Dominic Rayburn could, I've no doubt. And he doesn't intend . . .' She stopped awkwardly but Marie smiled warmly at her.

'Chérie,' she said, 'take confidence, and not only from your new clothes. You are the woman you are. If he cannot or does not approve, perhaps the fault lies with him.'

After Marie had gone, Stephanie wandered around tidying up, but with a thoughtful look in her eye. And it was as she stood with a beautiful cream silk nightgown in her hands that the door swung open to Dominic using his key.

'Now that,' he drawled, strolling forward, 'is an improvement on your everlasting cotton pyjamas. And these.' He picked up a delicate, almost-all-lace black bra from the bed and ran it through his fingers. 'You have let yourself go, Stephanie.' His eyes glinted.

She folded the nightgown up and put it in a drawer, her hands not quite steady. 'There's a lot riding on this,' she said huskily. 'Besides which, you're paying.'

'So I am,' he replied softly. 'If you can match the mood to the gilding of the lily, it will almost be worth it.'

'I thought you preferred me fighting—you,' she countered.

He looked amused and said idly, 'Things can always change. Have you had *any* fun today, acquiring these things?'

The question took Stephanie by surprise. 'I...' she paused '...yes, I have,' she said honestly. 'Marie understood my aura as well as my...' She broke off.

'Your "situation"?' he queried acutely.

'Yes,' Stephanie said baldly.

'Did she give you any woman-to-woman advice, I wonder?'

'As a matter of fact, she did.' Stephanie shrugged.

'You explained our curious marriage to her?'

'It came as some surprise to her to find out that you were married apparently—she,' Stephanie said with an effort, 'in common with most people, probably couldn't help feeling a bit curious.'

'I'm sure a lot of people do,' he agreed. 'My mother most notably,' he added drily. 'In fact she's quite bewildered and hurt and, I regret to say, keeps wondering audibly what kind of a woman you are when you won't live with me and won't even meet her. But then, so do I—wonder what kind of woman you are.' His look was ironic.

'So you keep telling me,' she said steadily. 'Marie, on the other hand, takes a more practical view. She seems to understand how marriages of convenience come to be made.'

He smiled faintly. 'Does she, now? Well, what kind of practical advice did she give you?'

Stephanie opened her mouth, shut it and considered, at the same time clinging to her composure. She said finally, 'I think I'll leave you in suspense there, Dominic. Does our bargain include what goes on behind closed doors? And does it start now or tomorrow morning?'

He thought for a moment, his eyes not leaving her defiant expression, then he said meditatively, 'Tomorrow, I think. We'll make a whole new beginning when I pick you up all dressed in your new clothes and playing your new role. Unless you'd like to spend tonight—rehearsing?'

'No, thank you,' she said stiffly.

'Very well—don't burst a blood vessel trying to keep a check on your temper in the meantime, will you? Goodnight, my beanpole wife,' he added sardonically.

Of course sleep eluded her until the early hours of the morning, as she fought and battled with herself for some rationalisation of what she'd committed herself to, some game plan to enable her to carry it through, some antidote for the terrible tension that was affecting her co-ordination—she'd dropped and broken a glass on the bathroom floor but not been surprised. Under strain she always became clumsy and uncoordinated.

But nothing presented itself to her and, to make matters worse, the old memories came back to plague her. Memories of her last year at school when she'd been accorded the signal honour of being appointed school captain. An honour that hadn't, however, quite bridged the gap that existed between her and a few of the girls—not all by any means, she always reminded herself scrupulously, and possibly less if I hadn't had a chip on my shoulder by then, but for twelve years Melissa Rayburn and her little clique made me feel raw, an outsider, a have-not, and as if I couldn't possibly mix with the likes of her. Then, that last year, she produced her brother because her parents were overseas and he was standing *in loco parentis*...

She sighed and turned over restlessly, desperately wanting not to remember and wondering why, five years later, she should still remember so clearly. It hadn't been her first crush, nor was she alone—the entire senior year was smitten—but she'd never had a boyfriend; there'd been so little time in her life and all that was spare she'd devoted to her growing fascination with art and her desire to paint. Another problem had been the lack of any woman to turn to for advice in the matter of clothes or to reassure her she was not as much of a gangling beanpole as she thought. But then it had not acutely worried her either—again because of a lack of time, and her determination to repay her father for all he'd spent with a good Senior Certificate; but it had sometimes struck her as ironic that she should be so alive to colours and style and form as they came from her paintbrush yet present such a capable and dull image to the world... The first time she'd laid eyes on Dominic Rayburn had changed all that.

It had been at a school concert and she'd suddenly become acutely discontented and unable to wrench her mind from this dark young god of twenty-four with his amused grey gaze and often wry look at being cast in the role of his sister's guardian. And she hadn't known what would be worse, to have him notice and dismiss her, or to be beneath notice at all.

To make matters worse the first time she had come to his notice had been due to her own incredible clumsiness...

She was the only girl to ride out of the school gates that afternoon, laden down not only with her bag and tennis racquet but also a small packet of groceries which she'd asked permission to slip out and buy during lunch hour so her precious study and painting time would not be interrupted. Just as she rode out of the gates, Dominic Rayburn turned his sleek sports car into the drive and, although there was plenty of room, Stephanie's bike wobbled for a few feet then she lost control and crashed into a lamppost.

Of course he stopped, and was unable to hide the amusement that crept into his eyes as he stared down at her horrified expression and the tangle she lay in of long, long legs, school books and groceries—including a burst packet of sugar.

'Are you hurt?' he queried immediately, though.

'No!' Stephanie denied, although she'd had no time to find out. 'No, I'm fine!' And to demonstrate she started to scramble up, only to sit down again with a faint gasp of pain.

'Your ankle?' he said acutely.

She bit her lip. 'Yes, but I don't think it's serious—I'm in a worse mess because of the sugar,' she added with a pale smile as she brushed at her blazer.

'Do you usually carry the groceries to and from school?' he asked, rescuing a jar of peanut butter from the gutter.

Stephanie blushed. 'No. Look, you don't have to worry; I'm fine really and Melissa will be waiting for you . . .' She stopped and frowned. 'Except that I think she might be playing netball this afternoon; it's an away match and I'm sure she was on the team—but perhaps I've——'

But Dominic Rayburn swore beneath his breath and went on packing her books into the bag. 'No, you're right—she told me this morning but it slipped my mind. I should really get her to write it all in my diary, shouldn't I?' He looked up and smiled at her, a smile that took her breath away, and went on, 'I don't believe we've met although you seem to know who I am but . . .' his gaze rested on her captain's badge. ' . . . I do believe I've heard about you.'

Stephanie shrank inwardly and looked away from that suddenly curious grey gaze. She mumbled something incomprehensible and, with an exceptionally clumsy effort even for her, attempted to haul her bike upright.

'Here, let me,' he murmured. 'Do you know,' he added, narrowing his eyes at the way she averted her hot face and continued rather gently, 'I don't believe you're going to be able to ride your bike home? The front wheel is buckled. How far away do you live?'

Stephanie jerked her gaze back to the bike and made an exasperated little sound.

'Perhaps I could give you a lift,' Dominic Rayburn offered.

'Oh, no,' she said agitatedly, 'it's not that far. I'll push it. And hang everything off it.' She smiled ruefully. 'Thank you for offering, though.'

All the same, five minutes later her bike was stowed precariously in the boot, her bags on the back seat, and she was installed in the front seat of his car.

'Are you sure it won't scratch your paintwork?' she asked anxiously as he slid in behind the wheel.

'Quite sure. I've put a car rug under it. How's the ankle?'

'Not bothering me a bit,' she said untruthfully.

'I should still put a cold compress on it,' he remarked, glancing down her legs to her ankle.

Stephanie bit her lip. 'This is very kind of you,' she said huskily.

'Not at all,' he replied and started the car up.

'I'm sure I'm scattering sugar all over your car, though.'

He glanced at her and grinned. 'This is really not such a disaster—by the way, I still don't know your name.'

She told him.

'Stephanie, then. But the bike wheel can be repaired, the sugar replaced and your ankle will mend. Therefore, I think you can afford to relax.'

Stephanie gripped her hands in her lap and tried to smile back.

'Just one thing,' he said after a moment, 'I'm dying to know why you were laden down with groceries in the first place.'

Stephanie hesitated, then told him, and watched one dark eyebrow shoot up as she did.

'So, you've had to grow up a bit ahead of your time, young Stephanie,' he said thoughtfully.

'I suppose so.'

'It embarrasses you?'

She looked out of the window and shrugged. 'No.'

He looked unconvinced but observed, 'You and my sister aren't in the same crowd, I gather?'

'No. It's the next turn to the left and the third house on the right.' An unprepossessing house and, to make matters worse, with a neglected garden, she thought with an inward sigh—all those dreams of impressing Dominic Rayburn must now be at nought.

Yet from somewhere she gathered the dignity to thank him quietly and to retrieve her possessions without further droppage or spillage and was only anxious for him to go.

Which he did, with a wave and a grin and a reminder to take care of her ankle. But she didn't study or paint that afternoon.

It was a month later and towards the end of their school year that the invitation came. Melissa Rayburn had never mentioned the incident and Stephanie had thought she'd put her dreams about Melissa's brother firmly behind her but, for the first time, Melissa invited the whole class to her party.

A party at the Rayburn mansion in Ascot—bring a boyfriend if you've got one, dress casually and tell your mums Dominic will be there to keep an eye on us.

Whether that was much consolation to any of the mums who were privy to their daughter's daydreams about Dominic Rayburn was debatable, but Stephanie guessed correctly that not one of her classmates would decline although she herself would.

But she didn't. In the end some small embers of *her* daydreams flared up again and she went—only to regret it almost from the start. She was the only one without a boyfriend, to begin with, and her outfit, which she'd given much thought to and liked before she arrived, was too simple. She'd also broken into her savings to buy some make-up but decided she couldn't be applying it properly and gone *au naturel* in that department with her hair tied back simply, to find that most of her classmates had transformed themselves into junior versions of *Dallas* or *Dynasty* stars and that their ideas of casual wear were designer jeans, silk blouses and high-heeled boots.

By the time all this struck her it was too late to retreat and she didn't know that, to a discerning eye, the soft chartreuse of her blouse and matching full cotton skirt highlighted her coppery hair and greeny eyes and accentuated her pale skin. She felt too awkward to have any idea that she looked youthful, fresh and long-legged, and on the tantalising brink of womanhood. She had no conception that her peers, for the most part, looked to

that same discerning eye like pouting little girls
playing at being grown up.

But she'd put on a brave face and indeed those
girls who liked and admired her had gone out of
their way to include her, and there'd been a few
spare boys so she hadn't had to sit like a wall-
flower. Then Dominic, who was obviously taking
his duties seriously, asked her to dance—his first
dance.

The almost breathless hush that fell over the party
for a moment didn't escape Stephanie's notice and
she could just imagine everyone thinking—why *her*?
Perhaps it didn't escape his notice either, she
thought from the glint of amusement in his eye.

'I see the ankle did mend as I predicted,' he said,
as he swung her into his arms.

'Yes...' she cleared her throat nervously. '...yes,
it did.'

'Enjoying yourself?'

'Oh, yes.'

'Then why are you looking about as troubled as
the last time I met you, sitting on the ground and
sprinkled with sugar?' he said softly.

She blushed. 'Am I? Sorry—I seem to have two
left feet at the moment; perhaps that's why.'

Dominic looked briefly over his shoulder. 'It
could be this bloody awful jungle beat they're
playing. Should we retire and get ourselves something to drink?'

Because nothing could be worse than stumbling
around under everyone's eye, she agreed, but, out
on the veranda alone with him in the soft darkness,
she was as tongue-tied as she'd been hamstrung, in
a manner of speaking.

So it was left to him to turn his back to the wooden railing and say as the silence lengthened, 'I can understand why they made you school captain, Stephanie.'

She blinked at him. 'You can?'

'Mmm. You may not be older but I'd say you're probably wiser than most of them.'

The sheer glow of pleasure his words brought her lit her eyes for a second then she grimaced.

'What?' he queried.

'It's not always a help to be capable and wise, if I am. Sometimes it makes you feel dull and different.'

'So it does bother you.'

'Yes, sometimes,' she said honestly this time.

He didn't pursue it but asked her what she intended to do when she left school and to her surprise she began to tell him about her dreams of art school and how she'd applied for a draughting job in the city council town planning office to help pay the fees as well as keep her, and as something to fall back on if she was no budding Picasso.

'You sound remarkably well organised,' he murmured. 'I wish I could say the same for Melissa.'

Stephanie was silent for a time, then she said shyly, 'What do you do?'

'I've just finished degrees in science and economics and am about to enter the blood-stained arena of the family businesses.'

Stephanie blinked and he laughed softly. 'I thought we Rayburns were renowned for our feuds.'

Perhaps it was that, she thought later, that was the real inkling she had of the gulf between them. Not so much the way he said it but what it im-

plied—*we Rayburns*. So much in those two little
words, she marvelled: confidence, money, power,
the right impeccable background. Unfortunately,
not five minutes later, Melissa managed to grind it
all in, in a way that was unforgettable.

She danced on to the veranda, saying imperi-
ously, 'Dominic! Why are you hiding yourself out
here?'

'I'm not hiding myself,' Dominic said wryly. 'We
were merely escaping your awful choice of music.'

'We?' Melissa turned and caught sight of
Stephanie and raised her eyebrows incredulously,
causing Stephanie to murmur something disjointed
and then to melt away and decide to take refuge in
the bathroom. But she took a wrong turning and
opened a door the led out on to the veranda but
around the corner so that, without being seen, she
could hear every word of the rest of their
conversation.

Melissa was saying, and not bothering to lower
her voice at all, 'I don't understand you, Dom! You
insist I must invite her to this party, which meant
I had to invite the whole class, then you single her
out, which is probably only getting the poor girl's
hopes up unfairly—can't you see she feels like a
poor relation or a freak at a side-show?'

'Melissa, you can be a right little bitch sometimes,' her brother replied pleasantly but with an
odd, sharp undercurrent. 'At least the poor kid . . .'

But Stephanie didn't stay to hear any more. She
slipped away and left the house and the party and
used the twenty-dollar note her father had pressed
on her in case of emergencies, although he'd been
going to pick her up himself at midnight, to get a

taxi home—after a long hike through the spacious, tree-lined streets of Ascot. Then there'd been her father's bewilderment at his daughter's un-scheduled arrival home to cope with and finally a telephone call from Dominic Rayburn.

'He wants to know if you're home,' her father said confusedly. 'Apparently they missed you—didn't you even say goodbye?'

'No. Just tell him I'm sorry and—thank you.'

'He wants to speak to you. Here,' her father said sternly. 'And then I want to know exactly what did happen!'

Stephanie sighed and took the phone. 'Hello.'

'Stephanie? Are you all right?'

'Fine, thanks. I'm sorry I left like that but——'

'You heard,' Dominic said flatly down the line.

'Well...' she bit her lip '...yes. But it doesn't matter—I'm probably a bit too sensitive, I mean...' She trailed off.

'How did you get home?'

She told him.

He swore and said grimly. 'You would have had to walk miles to find a taxi.' And she caught her breath because she had a sudden vision of the planes and angles of his face, of the arrogance of his expression which she'd never seen before but had guessed at. 'Look,' he went on in the same hard tones, 'I apologise for Melissa and——'

'Please,' Stephanie broke in huskily, 'could we just leave it? The least said soonest mended,' she added, thinking that she still had a few weeks of school to cope with.

Perhaps he read her thoughts, because he said abruptly, 'All right, but I am sorry. Can I speak to your father again? I'd like to apologise to him too.'

And that was that. Her father was supremely surprised to discover the kind of problems his children encountered, causing her to regard him with some oddly bitter resignation before her real affection re-established itself.

There were no repercussions at school—the Rayburn parents arrived home for one thing, so that at least she was spared the sight of Dominic, and Melissa, beyond the odd curious glance, neither apologised nor alluded to the party. But she doubted whether she'd ever forget, curiously not so much Melissa's words, but his own—the 'poor kid' and the stray streak of misguided chivalry that had prompted him to feel sorry for her.

It was a year before she saw him again. A year during which she worked conscientiously at the council and studied art at night, then was presented with the opportunity of a lifetime. An elderly friend of her father's, a lover of art, let it be known that she was contemplating a tour of Europe to visit all her favourite galleries and museums and cities but needed a travelling companion whose fare she'd pay. When it was suggested to Stephanie, she couldn't believe her luck and didn't have to think twice.

It was two nights before their departure that she ran into Dominic Rayburn at a restaurant where some of her friends from the council had taken her for a farewell dinner. It was perhaps fateful that she should be wearing the same chartreuse outfit—she'd found her interest in clothes had never been the same again—and also fateful that she should be feeling keyed-up yet a bit nervous and had had three glasses of wine.

Then the band struck up and someone asked her to dance, but only minutes later someone else tapped her partner on the shoulder and with a rueful grin he surrendered her into the arms of Dominic Rayburn.

The shock of it, of staring up into those amused grey eyes, the sudden proximity of the man who had aroused feelings in her that had never since been tapped, made her trip and gasp and brought a wry smile to his lips as he tightened his arms about her.

'Now, Stephanie,' he drawled, 'we're been down this road before. You really should take more care of your ankles.'

Of course she blushed and words eluded her as did the rhythm she'd been following so easily before, until he said, 'Perhaps we should sit down. Can I buy you a drink at the bar?'

'Yes, thank you,' she said raggedly. 'Sorry, but you were the last person I expected to see.'

'I hope you don't mean the last person you wanted to see,' he said with a lift of an eyebrow, 'although I couldn't really blame you.' He guided her across the floor to the dim recess of the bar.

'No! I mean ... I've forgotten about that night,' she said awkwardly, and wondered how true that was. She'd certainly made a determined effort not to dwell on it and had thought she'd succeeded. Yet being confronted with him now brought something of the rawness back. As for the rest of it, that hadn't changed at all, she discovered, glancing at him as he ordered the drinks. I might just as well be a silly, besotted schoolgirl—this is ridiculous, she mused painfully. I'm not tongue-tied and hot-handed with other people. Please God, give me . . . something!

It could have been the wine she was about to mingle with spirits that did the trick or perhaps God was in his heaven after all, because she accepted her drink and managed to say with a smile. 'This is a coincidence. How are you?'

'Very well indeed,' he replied. 'And actually the better for seeing you enjoying yourself. Are you with artists or town planners?'

'Town planners.'

'Did you do your art course?'

'Yes, I've just finished it.'

'So everything went according to plan—I'm not surprised.'

'Because you always knew how wise and capable I was,' she murmured, then grimaced. 'Until I ran away like a child.' But as his gaze narrowed she went on, 'How is the family business arena? As bloody as you expected?'

He shrugged and grinned and her heart beat faster because he was so good-looking but not only that—nice . . .

And incredibly they chatted together easily, mostly about him then about all sorts of things and it was with quite a surprise that she looked across at her table—not that anyone seemed to be missing her—and realised she'd been away for about an hour. But she was even more surprised at how well she'd handled the conversation so it hadn't been a question and answer session with him doing all the questioning. One thing that hadn't come up, though, was her imminent trip.

Then he gestured and mentioned that her party seemed to be breaking up and offered her a lift home unless she had other plans.

'Oh. No.' She stared at him for a moment. 'But you must be with someone and there's no need.'

'I was with a married couple and we were on the point of leaving when I saw you. They did leave. Besides, I feel I owe you a lift home.'

'No, you don't——'

'And this time you wouldn't have to worry about your bike or spilt sugar,' he said gravely.

'Well, thanks,' she said a little uncertainly and felt her stomach churn for some reason.

'I'll wait for you in the foyer.'

She went back to her table and made her farewells then retraced her steps rather hesitantly.

And, correspondingly, she was nervously silent in the car until he took a hand off the steering-wheel and put it over her clenched ones, saying gently, 'What's the matter?'

What was the matter? she wondered. The irony that she should see him again just before she was due to go away so there could be no hope of it amounting to anything? But that probably would have been the case anyway, she thought. All he ever felt for me was—pity. Why do *I* only have to see him to be possessed of hope again?

'Stephanie?'

'It's nothing,' she said, but to her horror she felt sudden tears in her eyes and he must have caught the sparkle of them because with a sudden frown he pulled the car up and switched the engine off.

'Tell me,' he ordered, sliding his arm along the back of her seat.

She sighed, a small desolate sound, and turned her face to his helplessly.

He stared down at her for an age, at the delicate bone-structure beneath her fair skin, her coppery hair plaited back tonight, at her narrow, slender hands and fragile wrists and the battered silver watch she'd worn for years that was her only adornment, if it could be called that. Until she saw a frown growing in his eyes and, to her despair, knew she'd given herself away.

It was that searing knowledge that brought her to life and, with jerky movements, she groped for the door-handle but he said, barely audibly, 'Oh, no, sweet Stephanie,' and pulled her into his arms. 'If that's the case, I have to tell you it is so with me as well. You always have had a...curious charm.'

Five years later, in the darkened bedroom at the Sheraton, Stephanie closed her eyes and wondered, as she had so very often over the intervening years, what had really caused her lapse in just about everything that night. Could she, in all honesty, blame the wine mixed with spirits? Or was it that the attraction he'd always held for her had simply refused to be denied recognition and had led her to that incredible but calm resolution that this, somehow, was her destiny? Then held her to it despite his surprise and, at first, reluctance.

Or perhaps, after all, she reflected, it had been the deep inner knowledge that while he might find a curious charm in her she was not the one for him—a knowledge that was mixed with the strange but strong conviction that by surrendering her virginity to him she would both break the bonds of this surprising passion and be able to grow from it, to be the woman she longed to be and be able to go forward as one even without him...

Whatever, fate had conspired with her—her father was away and not due home until the next day and her brother spending the night with a friend. Nor had there been any begging and pleading, only the way her mouth and body had responded to him, the look in her eyes which had perhaps deceived him a little—the mature accept-ance that she was, on that night, ready for love, his love.

She remembered it so well, the way he'd stared down at her body, at her breasts which were not as small as the rest of her might have led him to be-lieve, at the rippling, glinting fall of copper hair that she'd released, and she'd seen in his grey eyes then the unmistakable desire for her which he had not then been able to control.

He'd left her very early and they'd both been withdrawn and said little even before her father, who always rose at the crack of dawn, had rung to assure her he would be home that evening—her last in Australia for some months. Which had not only made her feel guilty but caused her to wonder why she still hadn't mentioned it to Dominic. But they'd said so little and her serene certainty of the night had dispersed in a growing cloud of confusion.

Then fate had intervened. She'd made herself go into town to collect her traveller's cheques and, coming out of the bank, she'd seen Dominic leaving the building by its main entrance accompanied by a beautiful, dark-haired girl in a red outfit; a glossy, elegant girl full of confidence and vitality. They'd walked to the kerb, obviously looking for a taxi, and, in the few minutes' wait, Stephanie had watched and seen them talking, then when the taxi pulled into the kerb Dominic had put his arm round her shoulders and the brunette had looked up into his eyes and raised her mouth for his kiss.

She'd walked away hurriedly and gone home to pack.

But he'd come, in the afternoon, when she was still alone in the house, and in her hurt and the inevitable tumbling down from the clouds of whatever had possessed her the night before she'd taken refuge in a kind of cold arrogance and they'd had a conversation she was never to forget...

It was a full two minutes before she nerved herself to answer the door, knowing it was him, then for an age they stared at each other wordlessly until a tinge of colour crept into her fair skin—over the whole of her body, she felt. She turned away abruptly but he caught her hand in a hard grip. He also said with a frown in his eyes, 'Is this remorse?'

She could feel the colour draining away, leaving her very pale, but she held her head high as she said, 'No—but it is goodbye.'

'*Goodbye,*' he said softly.

'Yes, I'm afraid so. I forgot to tell you, but I'm going overseas tomorrow.'

'Forgot?' The incredulity in his voice was now tinged with a sardonic undercurrent. 'How interesting—there was something else you forgot to tell me, wasn't there?'

She was silent.

'Stephanie?'

Still she said nothing.

'Something you could rightly say I should have asked—or even guessed, but you had changed.' His eyes captured hers.

She bit her lip then said carefully, 'If I'd wanted you to know, I would have told you.'

'Why wouldn't you have wanted me to know you were a virgin?' he countered. Then with a piercingly cold grey glance, he added, 'What the hell is this all about, Stephanie?'

She took a deep breath and suddenly her own gaze was cold. 'It was about two people who experienced a physical attraction and—consummated it. That doesn't mean you've fallen in love with me any more than I've fallen in love with you.' She said it without a tremor. 'It certainly would be stupid for me to make it into anything more and lose this trip, which is an opportunity of a lifetime, or for you to lose any sleep over it. Perhaps...' her lips moved into a semblance of a smile '...it was not much more than an experience in...slumming for you and...' she paused because her voice was getting shaky '...and——'

But he broke in derisively. 'Slumming? Did you have this all worked out before we...? You're an incredibly fast worker, Stephanie,' he drawled.

She set her teeth. 'What did you have in mind, then?'

He stared at her. 'I actually had in mind getting to know you better.'

She flinched inwardly but said quietly, 'Thank you, but I'm sure it would be pointless. Look...' she glanced away briefly then back '...it happened and, if it's any consolation, I don't usually mix my drinks. Could we just leave it at that?'

'Let's just see if I've got it right,' he murmured. 'You were drunk and feeling sexy and I just happened to be on hand—that's *all* there was to it?'

His tone stung her to the core and she was silent for a moment, battling a mixture of guilt, shame and anger. Misdirected anger, she knew, but could not help, at the image his words conjured up. Yet the alternative was to tell him the truth and there was just no solution she could see for what the truth would reveal. 'Yes,' she said coolly.

'You know, I underestimated you,' he said softly. 'I thought you were rather wise and mature; I didn't realise you were also cold-blooded—oh, speaking figuratively. Physically you're something else again. And I have to admit I'm quite floored and there seems there's not a lot more I can say, except to wish you well on your apparently chosen career of one-night stands, unless...' He stopped and stared at her as she clenched her hands together suddenly. 'Is this some kind of Freudian revenge for what you suffered at Melissa's hands?'

'That would be ridiculous.'

'My dear Stephanie, we are often ridiculous where our pride is concerned——'

'Perhaps,' she broke in swiftly, 'you should give a thought to *your* pride at the moment, before you pass judgement on mine.'

The sudden blaze of anger in his eyes made her swallow but she stood her ground and, because she was embattled but could see no way of retrieving anything, it was undeniably pride that made her add, 'Really, this is no big deal. I thought men understood better about one-night stands than women even.' She raised her eyebrows quizzically at him.

There was dead silence for about a minute, the kind of menacing silence that was echoed not only in his expression but in every line of his tall body. But it was more, it was an unspoken contempt that both shrivelled her and numbed her into the kind of despair that glazed her features to an expressionless mask.

'All right,' he said through his teeth at last, 'so be it. If, only by some mischance, I'm sure, you find yourself pregnant, what will you do?'

Stephanie came out of her frozen daze with a start. 'Th-there's not much chance of that, is there?' she stammered.

'Didn't you do biology at school?' he asked with ironic, savage impatience.

She realised her heart was suddenly pounding wildly and she tried to count in her head. 'Well...' she licked her lips '...well, I doubt it.'

'Good,' he said abruptly. 'But doubting it was never much of a safeguard, so I'm told. Which means we could both have a few anxious days ahead and I guess, Stephanie, therein lies the flaw to your spur-of-the-moment... activities. You really ought to be better prepared, you know. What will you do?' he said harshly.

'If you mean would I let you know——'

'Don't you think I'd have the right to know whether I was populating the world in my image?'

He stared at her grimly. '*If* that's how you decide to handle it, which I have to doubt.'

'I...' Her tongue tied itself in knots. 'I...would let you know,' she said barely audibly at last.

'How kind you are. Well...' his mocking, contemptuous gaze slid over her from head to toe '...that seems to be that. *Au revoir*, Stephanie.'

In a few days she'd known she wasn't pregnant and that final knowledge had caused her to sigh inwardly—a strange, shuddering little sigh—and made her distracted and clumsy for the rest of the day until her kindly, elderly companion had concluded she was feeling homesick.

She'd agreed but decided she had to get her act together, and succeeded outwardly. But one thing had come from the silent suffering she'd so resolutely put a bright face on during their slow, stately amble through Europe. She'd found that her perceptions were oddly more acute and it had occurred to her that if she'd achieved nothing else she *had* broadened her consciousness and sharpened her senses so that the beauty of the art they saw, the mastery and colours, seemed to engrave themselves on her soul and fill her more than ever with a burning desire to paint. She had matured, although the cost had been higher than she'd ever dreamt it could be, and there were times when she yearned to be able to turn back the clock. Times when she had to tell herself that it had been part of her growing up and, partly because of the way she'd *grown* up, had to be lived with and learnt from.

She'd learnt some more when she got home to find her father on the brink of marrying Nan and in the next few years when together they'd made a proper home for her and Mike at last. She'd learnt about love and affection and tenderness between two people and she'd even felt vindicated to an extent. But, perhaps most importantly, she'd learnt to recognise the passionate, unexpected side of her nature that, although it had led her in error to Dominic Rayburn, was also the core of her artistic talent.

She'd gone back to town planning part-time and painted in every spare minute, and if she thought about that night at times when she couldn't censure her thoughts the pain of it was tempered by all she'd learnt.

Then her father had died and not long afterwards her brother had made his unsuccessful bid to redress the balance between his financial status and that of those people he'd grown up with—at least her father hadn't lived to see it, she sometimes thought, and she also thought, Is it because we're twins that we have a different form of the same chip on our shoulder? Mike has this weakness and I perhaps excessive pride?

Nothing could have made it easier for her to face Dominic Rayburn, but that thought had made it even harder. Added to it had come the slow realisation that he seemed to be the one and only man who could distract the passionate side of her nature from her art, could arouse it still in spite of everything.

*   *   *

She fell asleep the night before she was due to go to Hayman Island with nothing resolved, no plan of action formulated—nothing beyond the hollow knowledge that she'd probably look a wreck in the morning despite her brave new clothes.

CHAPTER THREE

'WE FLY to Hamilton Island and transfer to the *Sun Goddess* which takes us to Hayman—you look tired,' Dominic said abruptly. 'I suppose you've been up half the night wrestling with your conscience.'

Stephanie smoothed the jacket of the beautiful vanilla trouser suit she wore with a yellow-gold blouse and shrugged.

'Well, at least in other respects you look the part,' he said impatiently and dropped a slim velvet box into her lap. 'These should complete the picture.'

They were sitting in the airport lounge surrounded by other travellers and she felt a sudden stinging urgency to toss the box back to him contemptuously, as her swift, narrowed, veiled glance must have told him, because he said with an ironic little smile, 'You can give them back to me when we part, if that helps.'

'It doesn't but I will,' she retorted, and opened the box. Her hands stilled and her eyes widened at what she saw. Only three pieces but each exquisite and each worth a small fortune. There was a Chopard watch on a bracelet band with five 'happy' diamonds floating around the face, a delicate gold chain necklace and an emerald and diamond engagement ring.

She looked up at last and said tautly, 'I salute you on your taste but I hope they're insured. You could probably feed a family of six for a year on their worth.'

'They are. They could also keep you for quite some time, or hadn't that occurred to you?'

'Unfortunately, I have this inbuilt aversion to being "kept". I thought we'd established that.'

They stared at each other until he said softly, 'Stephanie, we made a bargain. Why are you turning these...' he lifted the ring from the box '...which are supposed to help you feel the part, into such an issue?'

'Because nothing, least of all these,' she replied, 'will make me feel the part. In fact they make me feel the opposite and having them dropped in my lap in this manner and this place contributes to making me feel the opposite.'

'Which is?' he queried.

'Kept, bought, manipulated, used—I could go on but I won't,' she said steadily, then in suddenly frustrated, exasperated tones, she added, 'Don't you understand?'

His mouth hardened. 'Would any other time or place have been more acceptable? How about before one of your compulsory beddings—well, you could be right. Perhaps I should have chosen then, after I'd taken your clothes off. The chain would look rather unique over your bare, beautiful breasts.'

Stephanie looked around desperately, her cheeks growing hot.

'And they are beautiful,' he said barely audibly, 'and quite surprising——'

'Stop it,' she whispered.

'And particularly sensitive,' he said in a dry, normal voice. 'Don't look so embarrassed. We could be discussing the stock market for all anyone cares. Are you going to wear these?'

'For all you care,' she said bitterly. 'Yes, I will wear them. But only to ensure the success of our bargain.' She stared defiantly into his eyes.

But that was a mistake, she discovered, because he said then with a faint frown, 'How *would* you define our relationship, Stephanie? You use words like kept, manipulated, et cetera, but I don't knock you on the head and drag you into my bed, so are they valid?'

'*You* made it very clear you expected me to sleep with you when you wanted it or Mike went to gaol. It's quite simple,' she said coldly.

'It might be to you; it's about as clear as mud to me,' he commented. 'Because you make love to me with such passion, you see, albeit angry passion but nevertheless... You arrive when summoned and leave me in no doubt you're doing it under duress but once we—well, put it this way, put us in the same room with a bed handy and I only have to touch you to start the melt-down.'

Stephanie looked down and felt her heart beginning to pound. She said with difficulty, 'This is an impossible conversation——'

'It's a slightly impractical place to be having it, I agree...' his eyes glinted '...but I'm interested and I seem to have got you off the bit, verbally, so let's not waste the opportunity. Explain it to me, Stephanie.'

She took a breath and turned back deliberately. 'Don't think I haven't asked myself...this,' she said quietly. 'Because it's no cause for joy to me that you can make me want you when I despise your ways and means, so I have had this out with myself and I'll tell you my conclusion—I hope it brings you more comfort than it has me,' she said ironically and paused. 'I think I must have an oddly constructed personality. There is a part of me that...' She shrugged and wondered how to go on.

'A very sensual side of you, Stephanie?' he offered.

She grimaced. 'Yes. It must have something to do with the artist in me, I think. So far, only you seem to activate it.' She moved her hands restlessly. 'I see it as a weakness and certainly over the last year one that you've preyed upon. But of course I'm not blameless myself. That's what it is.'

Grey eyes stared into hazel and for a moment the bustle of Brisbane airport receded and they might have been alone on the planet—a younger Stephanie searching for a young Dominic Rayburn who had once embodied all her dreams and desires. Then she swallowed and veiled her eyes and the moment was broken.

He frowned faintly. 'So now you write it off as food for your art?' he said drily at last.

'Something like that,' she agreed abruptly.

'But why only me?'

She lifted her shoulders. 'I've been married to you lately. This odd affliction I have doesn't necessarily mean I'm promiscuous.' Her tone was suddenly weary.

'What about before we got married?'

'I managed to live without it.' She looked at him defiantly.

'Do you think you'll be able to live without it when we are no longer married?' he asked with a narrow, intent look and a twist to his lips.

'Yes—I think they're calling our flight,' she answered with an upward glance at the gate.

'How expedient,' he murmured but with a rapier-like glint in his eye. 'So.' He glanced down at the ring he held, then he dropped it back into the box and said, 'You don't have to wear them if you don't want to, but I see you're not wearing your old watch.' He stared down at her slender wrist then lifted his eyes to hers.

She coloured slightly and said awkwardly, 'It didn't seem to fit. I have it in my bag.'

'I thought about that watch, you know, when I bought this.' He fingered the Chopard with an oddly wry look. 'I thought it must have been a great watch to have lasted so long. You've worn it ever since I've known you, Stephanie.' His gaze held hers captive.

'Yes...'

'Ever since you rode your bike into a lamppost, in other words.'

Her lips parted and the colour mounted in her cheeks. He watched it and waited.

'Then... then it's probably time I did make a change,' she said disjointedly. She bent her head and took the Chopard and fumbled with the catch. Anything to get away from that probing gaze, those memories.

The *Sun Goddess*, a flagship of Hayman Island, arrowed her sleek lines through the island-studded waters of the Whitsunday Passage but at least two

of her passengers appeared unimpressed by her
beautiful lines and sheer luxury. Stephanie had slept
for most of the flight and accordingly been drowsy
and disorientated during the transfer from the
plane.

Once aboard, Dominic had suggested they take
their welcoming champagne to the top deck—about
the only thing he'd said to her since leaving
Brisbane. But it was refreshingly windy on the top
deck and lightly overcast and because they were so
high up it was fascinating to watch the different
patterns of silvery light on the water.

It was also as if there was an invisible wall between them until Stephanie, suddenly wide awake
and conscious of the bargain she'd made, tried to
break through it. 'Is this one of yours?' she asked,
about the boat.

'No. Built in Western Australia, I believe.'

'Is it anything to do with boats, this trip to
Hayman?'

He glanced at her. 'What makes you think it's a
business trip?'

'I can't think what else you would need me for,'
she said honestly. 'Is it?'

He considered and she watched him and recalled
the effect he'd had on the stewardesses on the plane
and the two groomed, attractive girls who had
handled the check-in procedure on the boat—on
most women, she reflected. Even now, sitting back
with the wind ruffling his hair, in a lightweight pale
grey and blue checked suit with a collarless knit
shirt, looking totally uncommunicative and uninterested, it was there, the magnetism of a superb
male animal.

'It is business but not with Hayman. We're meeting an American who's invited me up here to discuss an order he might place with Rayburn's—a very lucrative order.'

'I still don't see why you need me—but be that as it may,' she said and changed tack. 'He's chosen a lovely part of the world to do business.'

'Yes.' His grey eyes rested on her face. 'Ever been up here before?'

'No, and I'm only sorry I promised myself not to even look at a canvas for weeks now.' She gazed around ruefully.

'Because of this—us?' he said with a lift of an eyebrow.

'No. I appeared to have run out of inspiration but perhaps all I needed was a change of scene.'

'Or needed me?'

She tensed but made herself say evenly, 'Could we have a break from that for a while? We seem to have given it a pounding lately.'

He smiled unexpectedly. 'We do. But we have come up with some new aspects, you must admit. Such as my being the source of your artistic inspiration or something like that,' he said with a glint of mockery, 'which made me wonder.' He shrugged and added before she could speak, narrowing his eyes critically on the gold chain and ring she'd put on as well as the watch, 'It was quite a challenge choosing the right adornment for you, Stephanie, considering that I prefer you without any, which means that, in a way, we agree on that sensitive subject—possibly a first for us.'

'We *don't*——'

But he overrode her casually, 'What puzzles *me* is why I hold that preference—you see I can't put it down to my art,' he said guilelessly, 'but then again, your fascination was always different and difficult to pin down so I'm afraid I can't reciprocate in the way you have today. Sorry.'

'Perhaps I was right in the first place,' she said with difficulty as his wandering gaze rested on her mouth, and for a moment she longed to hit him.

'Right about what?' His lips barely moved.

'From time to time you enjoy slumming.'

He grimaced. 'I never did call it that, if you recall, but you might be right about something else. Let's give ourselves a break. How's your stepmother?'

Stephanie stared at him. 'She's fine,' she said uncertainly, but added, 'Although she's surprised I agreed to this, but then I didn't tell her the whys and wherefores.'

'And Mike? Does he know you might be let off the hook soon?'

Stephanie shrugged her slim shoulders. 'No. You probably see more of him than I do these days. No, he . . .' She broke off.

'Tell me.'

'He thinks I'm mad,' she said drily.

'Mad to make the kind of sacrifice you made for him?'

'He doesn't *know*——'

'He must know all is not well between us.'

'Yes, he knows that, but at the time we presented him with a *fait accompli*.'

'Ah, yes. You never told me how he reacted,' Dominic said. 'He certainly never offered to call me out nor does he show a tendency to want to punch me in the mouth when we meet.'

Stephanie winced but said tartly, 'Mike may have some glaring faults but you can't really blame him for being and thinking like a man. He was—at the time he was incredulous but intensely relieved and grateful. Now, and don't imagine I can't understand how difficult it must be to live feeling eternally grateful to someone, but, that aside, he still thinks it must have been something I...subconsciously wanted to do and that I'm mad not to make the best of it.'

Dominic laughed softly. 'Some things about your brother Mike will never change but in this he could just be right. I seem to remember expressing similar sentiments myself—no, don't look like that.' He lifted a hand and touched her cheek, a casual little gesture, and surprised her by saying, 'If you really want to paint, I'm sure we could get some materials flown in.'

Her eyes widened and her lips parted but he glanced over her head and said, 'This is Hayman coming up.'

Hayman was steep, Stephanie saw, its dark-green-clad slopes rising above a curved beach where the resort nestled. That was about all she was able to take in as the *Sun Goddess* berthed and her attention was distracted by two people on the jetty waving to them.

'Is...?'

'Yes. Ready, Stephanie?'

'Yes.'

* * *

The next half-hour was confusing but by the time they reached the cool, beautiful seclusion of their room, overlooking the pool and beach, some things had become clear to her and as the door closed behind Dominic she turned to him and was, somewhat to her surprise, laughing as she said, 'So *that's* it!'

He strolled into the main body of the room. 'You've made some sort of a deduction?' He looked at her dispassionately.

'Let me test it out,' she replied, her amusement cooling. 'Warwick Patterson is tall, distinguished and rather nice, he's obviously wealthy but . . .' she put her head on one side ' . . . in his middle to late fifties?' She waited until he nodded then went on. 'On the other hand, Veronica Patterson is only a few years older than I am, say twenty-eight at the most, she's gorgeous, his second maybe even his third wife—how am I going?' she asked gently.

His lips twisted.

'And she's got her eye on you. Hence *my* presence to divert her husband's suspicions and to safeguard this possible business deal.' She stopped and sat down on the bed abruptly. 'I wish you'd told me.' She stared up at him bleakly.

'Why? What difference would it make to you?' He shrugged. 'Don't tell me you haven't always suspected the worst about me, Stephanie.'

'But . . .' she found she suddenly felt cold ' . . . to use me as a decoy—how could anybody stoop that low?'

'There's a lot of money involved in this, Stephanie,' he said softly. 'I'd be a fool not to safeguard this deal any way I can.'

'She—is she really...? I mean...' She trailed off and a vivid picture of Veronica Patterson came to mind. Another brunette, quite tall, about her own height in fact, but that was the one similarity between them. Not only was their colouring poles apart but Veronica had contrived to display beneath a see-through blouse and a minuscule bikini an opulent, luscious figure, and of course the differences hadn't ended there. There was the matter of style, of that clear-voiced confidence, that sort of obliviousness to lesser mortals that she'd seen embodied in Dominic's own sister. Odd, Stephanie thought. Inherited or acquired? Not that it matters, just that I don't have it...

'Is she... hot to trot, not to put too fine a point on it?' Dominic drawled. 'She really is, Stephanie. Unlike you, she makes no bones about it. As a matter of fact, you two provide an interesting contrast in styles although you might just have an edge. Yes,' he said thoughtfully. 'The way you fight it gives it that little bit of spice. On the other hand, she does it illicitly, one could say, so perhaps that's how she gets her extra thrill.'

Stephanie put her hands to her face in an abrupt, jerky gesture. 'You... I can't *believe* you,' she said tormentedly. 'Of all the despicable...' She couldn't go on.

'Comparisons to make?' He smiled coolly. 'Or are you denying the extra thrill bit? Do tell me; I'm interested.'

'No, you're not, but I'll tell you this—I'm not going to stand for it. If you want to have an affair with Mrs Patterson go ahead if you already haven't but don't expect me to cover for you.' She glared at him.

'Oh, I didn't, not here,' he said lazily. 'As a matter of fact I don't carry on clandestine, illicit affairs with married women under their husbands' noses. Why bother? If that's what they want then they should "unmarry" themselves first or at least make their intentions known to their spouses in the form of a formal separation.' His eyes glinted.

Stephanie stared up at him with parted lips. 'I don't—I'm not sure if that's not the most utterly arrogant thing you've ever said,' she whispered.

He lifted an eyebrow. 'Why?'

'Because it's so typically male and you're also married,' she said and winced as soon as the incautious words were out.

'Am I?' he said softly. 'There are times when I don't feel it, Stephanie, times when no one could blame me for not feeling truly married——'

'Then you shouldn't have forced me into it, Dominic. You only have yourself to blame.'

'Well, my dear,' he said blandly, 'to be honest, between you and your brother I *was* beginning to feel a little hard done by, you see. An uncommon experience for me, I admit. All the same...' he smiled faintly ' ... I probably wouldn't have done it if I hadn't needed my grandmother's bequest or if I'd thought I could pin you down to a *de facto* relationship but, then again, I think my main motive was a sense of unfinished business between us, Stephanie. By the way, if I hadn't insisted on marriage would you have agreed to be my mistress?'

Stephanie licked her lips. 'That's academic now.'

He laughed. 'Oh, I think it would have suited your needs perfectly, but then I wasn't exactly aiming to please you. So much,' he added drily and significantly.

Stephanie shivered.

He saw it but made no comment. Instead he said, 'Well?'

'Well, what?'

'Now you know the score, what's it to be?' He turned away and opened his suitcase.

But do I know the score? she wondered. Do I know whether he's attracted to Veronica Patterson or not despite his cynicism on the subject of married women, any women really? Oh, God, perhaps I should just concentrate on getting myself out of this mess.

She said huskily, 'I gather the setting for our next encounter with the Pattersons is to be that magnificent pool outside. Would you like to go ahead while I unpack? I won't be long.'

'How very wifely,' he commented. Then he shot her a wicked glance and murmured, 'From your expression, dear Stephanie, I see it wouldn't be the right moment to expect any more wifely sentiments from you—I'll change in the bathroom, in other words.' He pulled a pair of swimming-trunks out of his case. 'By the way, if you're worried about your jewellery, we have our own safe.' He strolled over to a built-in corner cabinet and pulled the fretted doors open to reveal a television and video machine and, indeed, a safe. Stephanie blinked.

'All we have to do,' he went on, 'is come up with a six-digit code we can both remember.'

'That might be difficult. I don't remember your telephone number off hand and I'm quite sure you don't know mine. Birthdays?' She wrinkled her brow. 'I don't think we've ever exchanged that kind of information.'

He thought for a moment then knelt down and pushed some numbers on the keyboard, experimenting a few times, then he beckoned her over. The door was closed. He said, 'You work it.' And told her the code.

She hesitated then did as she was bid with unsteady fingers. The safe door opened with a faint whirring of the electronic mechanism.

'Think you'll remember those numbers?' he asked idly.

They were very close, both kneeling, close enough for her to see for the first time a few silver strands in the thick darkness of his hair with an odd little pang, although why she experienced that pang she couldn't say, particularly in light of this—if not a threat, undoubtedly a way of reminding her of her bargain.

She said huskily. 'Oh, yes. It's our wedding date.'

'Clever girl,' he said mockingly and stood up, helping her up at the same time and holding her imprisoned by the hand as he fingered the emerald ring. 'Don't be too long, Stephanie. The longer you put off taking the plunge, the harder it will be.'

His words stayed with her after he'd left, echoing in her mind as she unpacked. Which particular plunge had he meant? she wondered. The plunge into Warwick and Veronica Patterson's company? The plunge into her swimming-costume then the pool, or the plunge into pretending to be a loving wife? None of those, an inner voice told her. The other one that he *knows* I'm fighting, damn him, as I always do.

She was unpacking his suitcase from the stool at the end of the bed and she stopped and straightened and glanced around the room, at the beautiful eggshell and turquoise décor, the louvred doors that led to the veranda, and finally back to the bed, wide and smooth beneath the cover, and his other words came back to her. Put us in a room with a bed...

Tonight? she asked herself. Will he make me lay down my weapons one by one tonight? Will I know yet again the remorse, the useless anger, the disbelief because when I'm away from him I always manage to convince myself...it can't keep happening to me?

She lifted her gaze and stared unseeingly at the wall behind the bed as memories of one such night flooded her, the night he'd brought to mind with diabolical cleverness, their wedding night...

Once she'd accepted his ultimatum, he'd moved with incredible speed and she'd found herself looking 'down the barrel' of only a matter of days before she'd be Mrs Dominic Rayburn. Then it had been hours and she still hadn't been able to believe it, to believe that it wasn't some nightmare she'd wake up from. Even as he'd slid his wedding-ring on in front of a registrar and witness in the late afternoon, and kissed her deliberately on the mouth, it had been unreal.

And for the next couple of hours she'd been acquiescent and withdrawn, numb actually, still not really believing. He'd put her small suitcase in the boot of his car and driven her down to the Hyatt at Sanctuary Cove, a lovely colonial-style hotel set on the Coomera River. He'd suggested dinner when they arrived and she'd worn the same dress she'd got married in, not new—nothing in her case had been new. It had been a silent meal—it had been a silent few days on her part after an initial outburst of disbelief and anger that had amused him more than anything else and made no dent at all in his 'take it or leave it, that's my only offer' attitude— yet he'd not been perturbed, outwardly, and he'd suggested a walk through the village afterwards. But as they'd walked and window-shopped, a sort of inner trembling had started to build up and she'd tripped a couple of times so he'd taken her hand and held it in a hard grip and steered her back to their room ...

Once inside he'd only switched on one lamp and turned to where she still stood, just inside the door, and said mockingly, 'Anyone would think you were a virgin bride, Stephanie.'

She wrapped her arms around herself for a moment then made an effort to break out of the soundless morass of misery she was in. 'How did you expect me to be, Dominic?'

'I thought once it was done you might decide to make the best of it.'

'You don't know me very well, then.'

'In some ways I do.'

'No,' she insisted, 'not well in any way.'

'Do you know what I think we should do, Stephanie?' he said softly. 'I think we should con- centrate on the one way we...fascinated each other once. The rest might take care of itself then.'

She stared across the room at him, flushing faintly and suddenly tormented by memories—memories that she'd managed to keep at bay from the moment she'd walked into his office with her proposal on Mike's behalf and seen the hard, narrowed, speculative glint in his eyes as he'd scanned her from head to toe. That was how it had stayed over the past days; her stunned mind had blanked out that part of their past that she'd thought she could never forget—she'd been right, she realised now, it wasn't forgotten. How could she ever forget the giving of the only gift she'd had to give him, forget taking at his hands her passage to womanhood, the conviction that only he could do it, the lies later...? How unkind could fate be to bring her to this? She felt a hatred of his motives, even if she had invited his contempt, yet still this mysterious pull. This cruel, wakening awareness fuelled by those memories... It's not the same, she told herself desperately. This is a different Dominic Rayburn—you can't still feel the same way!

'Come here, Stephanie,' he said quietly.

She licked her lips. He was still standing next to the lamp but he'd taken off his jacket and loosened his tie and he looked disturbingly tall and frighteningly detached.

'No,' she whispered. 'I...I think I'll have a bath.'

He moved then, towards her. 'Later,' he said curtly.

'Dominic,' she said breathlessly, 'you can't do this. It isn't right.'

'It's perfectly right,' he murmured and stopped right in front of her. 'It's even legal and what we both want—what other criteria did you have in mind?' He put a hand on her shoulder then spread his fingers round the nape of her neck and into her hair, which she'd twisted up in a knot. 'Take it down,' he said with his lips barely moving but still that detachment in his eyes. 'I've never forgotten your hair. Or your body.'

'If that's supposed to make me feel better,' she said bleakly with a sudden shimmer of tears in her eyes, 'it doesn't.'

'Do you know, I don't particularly care how you feel right now, Stephanie? But one thing I do know, unless you've changed dramatically, is how you're going to feel. So if you want to fight, fight away, but I'm going to do this.' And he drew her shaking body into his arms and his mouth closed on hers.

She resisted as best she could but she was no match for him, and the tears that fell and the state she was in only contributed to her downfall. He simply wiped away her tears with his fingers and a crooked, mocking little smile and started to kiss her again. And, God help her, she thought at the time, when he unzipped her dress and slipped it off her shoulders and down her body there was this *knowledge* of him and his lovemaking in every fibre of her as if it had only happened to her yesterday and it was undeniable.

She woke as dawn was breaking. They hadn't drawn the curtains. And she lay without moving a muscle outwardly but her heart starting to beat heavily. Then she turned her head and discovered he was awake and watching her. She bit her lip and turned away convulsively—an action she was to question for a long time to come because if she hadn't done it would he have said what he did? Did she goad him into it after...?

Did I? she asked herself over a year later, with her cheeks warming as they always did at the memory of their wedding night and the way they'd made love. I don't know, although I also don't know why I should give him credit for anything, and if he hadn't said it what would I have done? Stayed and made the best of it instead of storming off after telling him that he'd made me marry him and he'd have to be content with that? How could I have stayed? But I'll never forget what he said... She closed her eyes.

'Don't tell me you're crying rape this time, Stephanie,' he drawled and sat up, 'because if you are it's a lost cause. Your actions speak much louder than words. You made love to me as much as I did to you. For that matter you also used words. Don't you remember saying please...over and over again, dear wife?'

It was laughter coming from across the pool that lapped right up to their veranda wall, and Veronica Patterson's unmistakable accent and clear voice, that broke into her painful reverie this time and she found she could picture Dominic, lean and tanned and beautiful in his brief trunks and the way Warwick Patterson's wife would be allowing her dark eyes to rest on him in a way she either hoped was a secret message or simply didn't care who saw.

'Well,' she said to herself and squared her shoulders, 'I don't know about damn Dominic and it's rather ludicrous to feel this way—must be the principle of the matter—but I'm *damned* if I'll let that woman walk all over *me*!'

CHAPTER FOUR

WARWICK PATTERSON was the first to notice Stephanie's arrival at the poolside.

In the same spirit of militancy she'd donned the bronzy pink lycra one-piece swimsuit of the two she'd brought, she had knotted a batik sarong with similar colouring about her waist and set a large, beautiful straw sunhat with an up-curved brim dead straight on her head—and been a little surprised that she'd been able to recreate Marie's artful tying of sarongs and correct angles for hats, and she approached the pool with long, fluid strides.

Warwick said warmly, 'Stephanie!' Whereupon Dominic turned, narrowed his eyes and stood up a fraction belatedly. Veronica, who was lying full length on a lounger offering her oiled body to the sun and whoever else was interested, squinted upwards, waved her fingers and didn't bother to sit up.

Warwick drew up a chair for her and said with his rather charming smile, 'But perhaps you'd prefer a lounger, Stephanie? Are you a sun worshipper like my wife?'

Stephanie grimaced down at her pale skin. 'I'm one of those people who goes pink and peels so I have to take it in easy stages.' She returned Warwick's smile with an unusually radiant one of her own and added, looking round, 'This is rather heavenly. Thank you.' She sat down and looked fully into her husband's eyes for the first time and her lips quivered as she saw they were faintly incredulous before he masked that expression adroitly.

He said, 'Would you like a drink?'

'I'd love one, darling,' she murmured and her gaze moved to a point over his shoulder. 'I do believe a drinks trolly is approaching.'

Veronica sat up and adjusted the back of her lounger. 'I wonder what this afternoon's offering is,' she said lazily. 'So, Stephanie, Dominic's just been telling us you paint.'

'I do,' Stephanie said wryly.

'Successfully?' Veronica queried, causing her husband to glance at her ruefully.

'Well, my paintings are selling now.' Stephanie shrugged and smiled faintly. 'That's one measure of success. The ultimate measure, the test of time and whether they'll be selling for a lot more in a hundred years, is also the ultimate irony, isn't it? One never knows, but I doubt it.'

'Because you're a woman?' Veronica said.

'That is strange, isn't it—no female Rembrandts or Van Goghs? I've sometimes...' her lips twitched '...thought of doing a George Sand but I think I might still lack the greatness.'

Veronica laid her head back dreamily. 'I can't imagine wanting to be a man for any reason on earth,' she said huskily.

There was a small, slightly awkward silence, during which her husband and Dominic exchanged amused glances and Stephanie thought, What can one say to that?

She was saved the necessity of saying anything by the arrival of the cocktail trolley and they all ordered the exotic concoction on offer served in balloon glasses.

Stephanie sipped hers and contented herself with looking around—the view was indeed something to behold. The pool was enormous and in fact two pools: an outer lagoon criss-crossed by wooden footbridges, and an inner freshwater pool. The two branches of the west wing with their colourful red awnings framed the pool but in the other direction, across the pattern of pool, sandy pink stone coping, wooden decking and terracotta bowls of bougainvillaea, was the real view—the turquoise waters of the Whitsunday Passage across to Hook Island through a date- and pandanus-fringed foreshore.

The air, Stephanie decided, was that balmy tropical blend of heat and humidity and was oddly soothing—something was oddly soothing anyway, she decided, because she now felt peaceful when she should be annoyed. Why? Annoyed, she reflected, because I think Veronica Patterson is going to go out of her way to subtly put me down... It would be odd if the peace and the beauty of this place defeated her honeyed little barbs...

'Oh!' She came out of her reverie, to find Dominic leaning across the table touching her wrist. 'Sorry. I was miles away.'

He grinned. 'How about a swim?'

'I'd love one!' She stood up lithely and stripped off her sarong. 'All the way round?' she said teasingly.

He stared at her with a wicked little glint in his eye. 'All the way, Stephanie.'

*   *   *

They did it in stages and a variety of strokes.

'This is a swimming marathon,' Stephanie said laughingly once. 'What we should really do is try to swim a little further without stopping each day.'

'Done!' he answered. 'But you're obviously not a bad swimmer...' He stopped and looked around wryly.

'It's all right, they're out of earshot—but you'll have to be careful not to give the game away,' she added innocently and set off in a fast crawl with a wicked grin of her own.

It was in that same spirit that she left the water finally and accepted the huge, fluffy towel pressed on her by an attendant. They made their way back to the Pattersons and sat chatting with them easily and with a carefree vivacity on Stephanie's part that surprised her a bit, until Veronica decided it was time to begin her preparations for the evening, and suggested they meet for dinner at the Italian restaurant, La Trattoria.

It even earned her a compliment from Warwick, her spontaneous gaiety. He said suddenly, 'I do believe the next few days are going to be a lot of fun with you here, Stephanie.'

She thanked him with a warm, genuine smile but couldn't help noticing Veronica standing up rather abruptly. Oh, dear, she mused, am I laying it on too thick? Why do I get the feeling I'm going to pay for that compliment? But actually I was just enjoying myself. She glanced at Dominic but his expression was unreadable.

*   *   *

It was not so when they got back to their room.

'Bravo,' he said softly, coming right up to her as she dropped her hat on the bed. 'That was very well done, Mrs Rayburn. May I salute you on an excellent performance?'

'I . . .' She stopped as he drew her into his arms and she realised what kind of a salute he had in mind.

'No—please,' she said raggedly but of course there was no sensation on earth for her quite like the feel of his arms around her, their cool, barely clad bodies touching, the way his glinting gaze rested on her trembling lips. She tried again, 'Dominic . . .' and brought her hands to try to push him away, only to be resisted easily.

'Stephanie?' he murmured in reply and when she couldn't go on he said, 'Know what I'd like? I'd like to take you back into the Pattersons' company looking languorous, sated and thoroughly made love to. You do look like that sometimes, you know. Pale and satiny but your eyes go darker and you move differently, as if you're dazed—and you're docile and dreamy——'

'Stop it,' she whispered. 'This *is* stooping incredibly low.'

'Is it?' His lips twitched in the faintest smile and he moved his hand to caress her back. 'Tell me why.'

'Because that's the kind of thing you shouldn't ask of anybody in . . .' she hesitated but made herself go on ' . . . in the cause of business and when things are all but over between us. To——' her voice shook '—to——'

'Make love would be immoral when things are all but over between us?' he finished for her. 'Your morals confuse me sometimes, Stephanie.' His gaze was ironic and she flinched visibly.

He waited for a moment but she couldn't speak. 'Tell me this, then—do you think things will ever be entirely over between us, Stephanie?'

She swallowed, pinned beneath his sardonic gaze.

He waited again and felt her shiver down the length of her body as his hands moved to her hips, and he smiled. 'Because for as long as we want to make love to each other I don't see how they can be. Incidentally, it wasn't for purely business reasons that I suggested what I did. I suppose it was something to do with a purely masculine, purely vain desire to have everyone know it was me this rather enchanting creature . . .' his gaze roamed her damp hair, still drawn back from her face in two combs and one thick plait ' . . . who has virtually blossomed before my eyes—sleeps with.'

'They would assume that anyway,' she said hoarsely.

'That's not quite the same thing as seeing the impact of it but you're right.' He released her thoughtfully. 'A rather base desire, no doubt. My apologies. We still have two hours to kill before we meet the Pattersons. How do *you* propose we fill them?'

She turned away from the mockery of his words and, simply for something to do, drew out the combs in her hair and started to unplait it. 'You could read a paper or watch television, relax, while I have a bath and dry my hair, decide what to wear.' She combed her fingers through the rippling mass of it as it came free. 'That kind of thing,' she said desolately and with a sudden sparkle of tears in her eyes that horrified her.

He watched her bent, averted head critically for a moment then she turned her back to him. 'You're crying,' he said with a frown. 'Why?'

'I'm not!'

'Wanting to, then.' He touched her hair then took his hand away. 'Stephanie?'

'I . . .' Her shoulders slumped. 'I'm a bit tired, that's all. It's nothing.' She closed her eyes and battled the treacherous tears, tipping her head and stretching her throat as if to stretch away the insidious tension that would soon have her tripping and dropping things, then she stilled as she felt his hands on her shoulders, massaging gently.

He did it for several wordless minutes and pushed her down on to the bed with the frown still between his eyes. 'Wait there,' he murmured as her eyes widened.

She sat with her hands in her lap and heard the bath running, but when he returned and led her to the bathroom the sight that greeted her eyes made her blink—a splendid bubble bath.

'Enjoy it,' he said wryly. 'Just don't lose yourself in it. I didn't realise how powerful the stuff was.'

She lay in the bath for an age, at first pondering the weakness that had nearly led her to tears, the unconscious yearning she'd expressed—had he guessed?—for things to be ordinary between them, for them to be like any other couple in the quiet times. Then she simply soaked in the scented frothy water and tried to relax. She washed and dried her hair and when she finally left the bathroom it was to find the louvred shutters closing out the darkness, the lamps beside the bed on and the room aromatic with fresh coffee. Dominic was lounging on the bed watching television in a twin of the fluffy bathrobe she wore.

'I decided to take your advice,' he said gravely.

'How was that?'

'It was great,' she said huskily.

'Come and complete the cure.' He indicated the other side of the bed. 'I don't know if you're a *Goodies* fan but that's what I'm watching. It's quite funny. Here, I'll pour your coffee.'

A few minutes later Stephanie was curled up on the bed beside him, sipping her coffee and, despite herself, chuckling softly.

'Feeling better?'

'Yes. Sorry.'

'No, I am. Until next time,' he said barely audibly and grimaced as she turned to look at him. 'There seem to be times when I can't help being a bastard where you're concerned in spite of some good intentions. Does it help to know that I do acknowledge that occasionally?'

Nothing helps, she thought, as they stared at each other. In fact it's the times when you can be so nice that make it so hard. She lowered her lashes and said, however, 'Yes.' She smiled faintly. 'This place is rather lovely, isn't it?'

He took his time replying and she was afraid to look up in case he was going to challenge her change of subject but he said finally, 'There's much more to see of it yet. They have quite an art collection here which you should enjoy and the gardens are almost works of art themselves. I'm sure there'll be times when Warwick and I get to business and you'll be able to potter around on your own.'

'I like him,' Stephanie said, relaxing. 'I mean he's not a typical...' She shrugged.

'Sugar-daddy?'

'Well, for want of a better expression, yes, and he doesn't throw his weight around.'

'No. What about her?'

Stephanie grimaced. 'There's probably no way we could like each other,' she said honestly. 'I don't think she's a woman's woman somehow and if she has got her eye on you it's just going to be a contest, isn't it? Although I have a slight advantage she doesn't know about.' Do I? she wondered as Dominic moved and she tensed but he obviously decided to let what she'd said pass. 'And,' she continued with her mouth curving wryly, 'in spite of yourselves, you and Warwick are going to be amused at the games we girls play, no doubt.'

He didn't deny it. 'That offends you?'

The curve of her mouth became a mischievous grin. 'Dominic,' she said gravely, though, 'if we girls couldn't indulge you men in these little things, the human race would have died out aeons ago.'

He laughed. 'Dear Stephanie—I'm quite chastened!'

'I wonder?' she murmured.

'Oh, I am. Well, seeing as we've sorted that out, should we gird our loins for the next session?'

Stephanie dressed while he was showering and in the process thought, I could get quite used to this. She chose a pair of soft jade harem pants with a matching cropped jacket and a tissuey gold cummerbund that emphasised her narrow waist. Gold shoes with small heels completed the outfit. Dominic came out of the bathroom as she was staring at herself in the full-length wall mirror and he whistled softly.

She coloured faintly and grimaced. 'I'd never have chosen it myself so I ought not to take much credit for it.'

'It's still you inside, showing it off,' he returned with a lifted eyebrow. All he wore was a towel slung round his hips and there were droplets of moisture on his broad, tanned shoulders.

'Yes, well,' she murmured, feeling her pulses starting to beat, 'I'd better complete the picture—if you've finished with the bathroom.'

'It's all yours,' he said with a lazy grin.

She applied her new make-up with hands that weren't quite steady and brushed her hair and tied it in her nape with a gold ribbon. When she came out of the bathroom, he was dressed and waiting in grey trousers, an open-necked white shirt, a navy blue blazer, and, privately, he took her breath away.

Damn, she said to herself as they left the room and walked through the orchid-studded flagged passageways towards the club lounge. And added an obscure warning—be cautious, Stephanie.

The Pattersons were waiting for them, Veronica glowing in primrose-yellow and apparently in a different mood as she eyed Stephanie's outfit and demanded to know where she'd got it—it was so chic! But she turned to Dominic almost immediately and confided plaintively that she was starving and wouldn't it be a good idea to eat early?

They all agreed and were soon seated in La Trattoria where once again Veronica chose to sparkle.

'Isn't it just perfect! So *authentic*.' She gazed around admiringly. 'Of course Rome is one of my favourite cities—it's so romantic.' She closed her eyes dreamily then opened them wide and focused them on Dominic. 'Do you and Stephanie have a favourite city? One with those special memories?' she asked huskily.

She knows about our marriage—the thought popped into Stephanie's mind. But how could she unless...? No, it's my imagination, she told herself, but how to answer?

Dominic answered with an easy smile. 'We do. It happens to be our home town.'

Veronica chuckled. 'Little old *Brisbane*? Fancy that. Well, tell me about it, then, and your lives there, how you met, how you live, how your marriage works, how many children you plan to have——'

'Veronica,' Warwick interjected warningly, causing her to pout at him and demand to know what was wrong.

'At the very least you're being inquisitive,' he said severely.

'And at the most, Warwick?'

Dominic intervened as Stephanie again wondered just how innocent all this was. 'We met when Stephanie was still at school, in fact. It would be true to say her legs got me in even then,' he said with a ghost of a smile.

A statement that caused Stephanie to colour and hope wildly that no one had noticed, and Veronica to lose interest. They were all saved by the arrival of the waitress and perhaps Veronica took Warwick's warning to heart because she behaved impeccably from then on and the conversation became general and genuine. But although she gave no cause for direct offence it didn't stop Veronica from being the life and soul of the party nor did it inhibit her from dancing when the band struck up, and charmingly appropriating Dominic for a solo tango which they did expertly and fluidly to the delight not only of the other diners but of the Italian band.

Nor, Stephanie discovered, as she applauded with the rest and watched Veronica, flushed and breathless and laughing as she and Dominic wove their way back to the table, could you deny that she was gorgeous and very spirited and that it might be a combination that was hard to handle.

She turned to Warwick on an impulse, to say something along those lines about his wife—not the hard to handle bit—but was arrested by his expression. Because Warwick Patterson was watching his wife approach with his heart in his eyes, with a mixture of pain and fatal fascination that told its own story.

Stephanie turned away and felt her heart go out to him as she thought that they might be two of a kind, or, at least, on the same kind of treadmill.

It wasn't long afterwards that she realised she was tired and tense again, as well as curiously sad, and she turned to Dominic, wondering how much longer he would want to stay.

Perhaps he read her eyes because in a surprisingly short time he'd extricated them, although their departure was aided by another American couple joining the table and showing no signs of flagging, to Veronica's delight.

But of course leaving the party doesn't solve my immediate problems, Stephanie thought, as they walked back to their room. What happens now? What will he...expect?

Of course she tripped thinking these thoughts, in her low-heeled shoes and over nothing at all.

Dominic took her hand and steadied her as he scanned the smooth stone floor. 'What was it?'

'N-nothing,' she stammered. 'I just get clumsy when I'm w—tired, when I'm tired,' she said foolishly. 'Don't you remember?'

'I do. Tired—or worried?' He swung her round to face him and his eyes were acute and cool.

Her shoulders slumped and she looked away.

'Stephanie.' His voice was soft but commanding.

'All right, worried,' she conceded, staring at the floor.

'About us?' The words were clipped.

'About——' she raised her head '—the forthcoming battle of the bedroom, as if you didn't know,' she whispered and her eyes were bleak. 'I'm sure there's going to be one.'

'Then let's get to it,' he said blandly. 'I'd hate to disappoint your expectations.'

She tried to pull her hand free as a burning flush travelled up her throat but he walked her unhurriedly yet inexorably to their door.

Inside, she stopped in the middle of the room with her head bent, her back to him for a moment, then she turned defiantly. 'If I've misread things, my apologies,' she said tautly. 'It must come from experience of you.'

He stepped towards her and there was menace in every line of his body, not overtly but in the very contained way he moved, like a jungle cat stalking... But his expression was entirely enigmatic and, because she knew him, *that* she also knew and feared.

He said, when they were only inches apart, 'Experience, Stephanie? How right you are. This is always a battle for you, isn't it?' His grey eyes raked her from head to toe deliberately and insolently in a way that she was no match for and recalled all the times she'd lain in his arms after just such a beginning as this.

Her lips trembled, although a spark of anger made her eyes glint gold. 'At least...' She stopped.

He smiled a cool, absent smile. 'Go on,' he invited. 'I take it you're going to parade your morals before me again? At least you fight this immoral desire we have for one another? Is that what you were going to say? Whereas I merely indulge it—— '

'*No*—I mean, that wasn't what I was going to say,' she broke in jerkily.

'Then do enlighten me,' he drawled.

At least I love you... She didn't say it. She fastened her teeth on her bottom lip and went hot and cold at the admission she'd made even if only to herself. How could it be true after everything she'd been through? She closed her eyes and turned away abruptly.

He laughed softly. 'As it happens your morals are quite safe tonight. I was fully proposing to

extend our earlier truce to the—er—battle of the
bedroom, as you so colourfully phrased it. Incidentally, that's nearly as good a phrase as your
other one—compulsory bedding, wasn't it?
Unless...' he paused '...you'd care to change your
mind and allow me to put you out of your misery.'

She swung round. 'Oh, God, you're a...'

'Bastard? Perhaps.' He shrugged. 'But at least
I'm honest, which you, my dear, for reasons known
only to yourself, are not. Sleep well—I'll relieve you
of my tormenting presence.'

'Where are you going?'

'Going? To find some more congenial company,'
he said with a lethal kind of gentleness. 'That
shouldn't be too hard.' He strolled out, closing the
door quietly behind him.

CHAPTER FIVE

STEPHANIE slept fitfully after several hours of dry-eyed, painful self-examination that included telling herself she *could* be forgiven for misjudging Dominic's intentions. She also told herself it was impossible to love a man who delighted in insulting her the way Dominic did—then she thought drearily that all her excuses were wearing a bit thin.

At dawn, when he still hadn't returned, she knew she couldn't lie there any longer so she pulled on her costume under shorts and a top and went for a walk.

It was a perfect morning with just a few wisps of cloud in the sky and a feeling of heat already in the air. There was no one about and at the far end of the beach she stripped to her costume and waded into the sea. Then she walked back, her body tingling but her heart as heavy as lead. She was still apparently the only soul up and about.

Not quite so, she discovered as she let herself into the room. Dominic was up and about.

He was standing at the doors to the veranda in the clothes he'd worn the night before, but with his blazer slung over a chair, and he would have seen her coming but he didn't turn until she'd closed the door and come right into the room.

When he did, she saw that his hair was ruffled and lying across his eyes and his jaw was shadowed blue. He looked, she thought, weary, drained and disenchanted and she tensed, waiting for the inevitable mockery.

But he said at last only, 'Shall we order breakfast?'

She blinked. 'Yes, if you like. It's still very early.'

He smiled, a bare twisting of his lips. 'It's later than you think. Warwick and Veronica arranged to hire—weather permitting—a yacht for the day for a leisurely sail around the islands and lunch on board. A day in paradise,' he said and the irony was unmistakable now. 'Even the weather's conspired against us.'

Stephanie took a despairing breath. 'I don't—they didn't mention this last night,' she said as a new thought struck her.

'Warwick did to me.' His eyes narrowed.

'Oh.'

'You sound disbelieving,' he murmured.

Stephanie clenched her fists. 'I . . . it doesn't matter.'

'But it does,' he insisted. 'How else would I have known, for example?' He stared at her coldly and challengingly.

Stephanie bit her lip and cursed herself for caring or even wondering where he'd spent the night, but the damage was done. 'If I did wonder,' she said steadily, 'whether by some stratagem you and Veronica got rid of Warwick and spent the night together, I'm sorry, but it did . . . just spring to mind.' She sighed and rubbed her brow. 'Look, Dominic——'

'No, you look, Stephanie,' he said quietly but so coldly that she shivered. 'For one thing, the way things are between us, what does it matter where the hell I spent the night? But for another——'

'It matters,' she said bitterly.

'Why?' he shot at her. 'Only yesterday you were telling me that you had a secret weapon against Veronica Patterson. I presumed you meant that it would be impossible for her to make you jealous seeing as you have no proper, *wifely* feeling for me but now——'

'I *meant* that whatever the circumstance,' Stephanie broke in urgently, 'I don't have to be made a fool of by that woman in front of others who have no idea what the circumstances are, anyway!'

'And if it was another woman?'

'If it was...was it?' she whispered before she could stop herself, or stop the way her face paled and her hands shook. But she made a supreme effort to redeem herself and said, also before she could stop herself, 'At least if it was, she won't be able to gloat publicly!'

'Then for your comfort,' he said drily, 'Veronica has nothing to gloat about.'

'But I think she knows,' Stephanie said abruptly and winced as he swore beneath his breath.

'She knows nothing,' he said precisely. 'If she's given you that impression, she's only fishing. It's her nature—either that or you're very sensitive, Stephanie, when you don't need to be, I would have thought.'

She licked her lips and stared up at him.

'And for your further information and comfort I found a couch in a deserted corner of a deserted lounge and, if you could call it sleeping, that's where I slept. Alone,' he said roughly. 'I doubt if I was detected by anyone least of all the Pattersons, so the illusion...' his lips twisted '...of our marriage is still intact. What's more we made a bargain—I'm sorry you're finding it so hard to keep but——'

'The really incredible part,' she broke in huskily, 'is why I should have to respond to blackmail in the first place!'

'You should,' he said softly, 'have thought of that years ago. Even before your brother got caught with his fingers in the till. It should have occurred to you when you used someone for your own purposes entirely that one day you might be similarly used yourself.'

'But,' Stephanie said, a bare breath of sound, 'it was only once. It was only... it couldn't have affected your *life* as you've wrecked mine. Was it such a crime?' A nerve beat in her jaw and her eyes were curiously agonised.

'By itself, no,' he said dispassionately. 'But you see, you've gone on compounding it, and perhaps the ultimate insult is that you persist in viewing me from some Olympian height of virtue as if you *never* slept with me once under false pretences and then as good as told me it was only an exercise in lust.'

Tears sparkled on Stephanie's lashes but she refused to allow them to fall. And something in her heart cried to her to tell him the truth but another voice in her brain sounded a warning—would he believe the truth after she'd closed so many gates behind her?

She said hoarsely, instead, 'If you're trying to say we're as bad as each other, if that's what you want me to admit then, yes, I do. I—it was a terrible mistake I made that night. Do you think I haven't had *years* to know that?' she said anguishedly. 'And—but what does that change? I did it. I...' her voice sank '...did it.'

'Why?'

The question was stark and her lips parted beneath the compelling power of his eyes. 'Because I am a cold-hearted bitch, probably,' she whispered and because her knees suddenly felt like giving way she would have sunk to the floor if he hadn't taken her by the shoulders.

'Go on. Is that all?' he commanded and his fingers dug mercilessly into her flesh.

'I don't know! I...maybe I did think it would be a private feather in my cap if I could have you for my first lover. Dominic Rayburn...' she grimaced but she was as white as paper '...whose sister had always ignored me as if I didn't exist.'

She saw his mouth thin. 'You went out of your way to deny that, Stephanie. Besides, it doesn't make sense.' He frowned, looking over her head as if into the distance, then he brought his eyes back to her face. 'Private feather? How much more effective,' he went on as if talking to himself, 'to go public—that would have been a real one in the eye for his sister——'

She broke in raggedly. 'I wasn't to know you'd be party to *going* public.'

Their gazes clashed.

'Then of course, it could have all b-backfired,' she stammered, thinking a little wildly that she was coming unstuck. 'I mean, it could only ever have been a temporary thing...' her voice shook '...to Melissa's delight, no doubt.'

'So.' He released her at last and she groped for the bed and sat down. 'It was that all along. You saw an opportunity and took it. Was that *private* revenge sweet, Stephanie?'

Her throat worked but she couldn't speak.

'Why haven't you taken the opportunity to flaunt our marriage before Melissa, then? Wouldn't that have been the ultimate revenge? Or are you getting it another way—by proving you don't need me even though I married you?'

'No. No,' she said bleakly. 'What's come since has all been *your* doing. I may have some faults but I'm not as conniving as that.'

They stared at each other and she saw that his face was pale too, and saw something in his eyes she didn't understand.

He opened his mouth but the phone on the bedside table rang. Stephanie hesitated then picked it up. It was Warwick.

'Stephanie!' he said genially. 'You are an early bird! I saw you taking your constitutional along the beach—is your husband up and about? By the way, did he mention we were thinking of taking a yacht out for the day?'

'He...yes!'

'Good. The weather report is excellent so here's what I thought: that we'd meet for breakfast in, say, half an hour and then it's anchors away. How does that sound?'

'It...' Stephanie cleared her throat and forced some enthusiasm into her voice '...sounds great, Warwick! We'll be there.'

But she put the phone down and buried her face in her hands for a moment before imparting the gist of the conversation to Dominic. It was little consolation that his face tightened and he swore quite explicitly on the subject of the Pattersons and their boating plans.

It was a perfect day for sailing. Sunshine and enough breeze to send the forty-foot yacht skimming gently along. The crew, a husband and wife team, were unobtrusive, but it wasn't long before Dominic was offered the wheel and as Stephanie watched she saw the tension only she knew about drain away as he handled the boat as expertly as its master and saw him revel in the sun and sky, the pale blue expanse of water, the peace...

In fact she found it hard to tear her gaze away from him, clad as he was only in a pair of shorts with his shoulders bare and smooth and a jaunty borrowed peaked cap on his head. Then she wondered if he was having the same effect on Veronica but Veronica seemed to be in a calm, passive mood and no sooner was she on board than she had chosen herself a part of the deck where she could sunbake in yet another bikini, and there she stayed, apparently oblivious to the rest of the world.

It was Warwick who explained ruefully that his wife was not a morning person and could be expected to remain comatose until lunchtime.

Thank the lord, thought Stephanie, then felt guilty and wondered if she wasn't even a bit envious. For she herself was not only incapable of relaxing but, as a precaution against the intensifying reflection of the water, was swathed in white linen, sun-cream and a concealing hat. A rather wry

smile curved her lips and since Dominic was oc-
cupied she turned to Warwick and together they
admired the wonders of the Whitsundays.

So the day progressed. They had a delicious lunch
on board and swam in the turquoise waters. Then
they headed homeward and the breeze freshened
sufficiently to delight any sailor's heart, the sails
sang and Veronica perked up as the skipper's wife
produced fresh piña coladas—and Stephanie came
to grief.

She was negotiating the steep ladder down to the
main cabin—she hadn't yet touched her drink—but
the yacht heeled, she lost her footing and crashed
to the cabin floor.

It was Dominic whose face immediately appeared above her, then he was down the ladder as
sure-footed as a cat as she lay winded and crumpled
up awkwardly and not sure if she'd broken every
bone in her body or was just imagining it.

'Stephanie...' He gathered her up. 'Oh, *hell*! Isn't
it time you grew out of this? Are you all right? Tell
me where it hurts!'

The skipper's wife had materialised beside him
and said with gentle reproach, 'For someone not
used to boats it could just have been the motion.'

But Dominic laughed briefly and Stephanie
shrank. 'You don't know my wife! She——' He
stopped exasperatedly and eased her away from him
but the tears in her heart translated to real tears
that streamed down her cheeks. 'I'm all right,' she
wept and was consumed with embarrassment at the
way the two gazes met above her soberly and concerned questions issued down the ladder well.

With no help from her they laid her on a bunk and Dominic ran his hands over her expertly while the skipper's wife talked soothingly.

'Nothing's broken,' Dominic said at last. 'Stephanie, can you sit up?'

She did with an effort and several deep breaths helped her to control the runaway tears. 'I'm fine.' She smiled feebly. 'I might have a few bruises, that's all. See?' She slipped off the bunk and stood up. 'It was more the shock of it than anything else and your thick carpet helped. Please, I'm sorry if I gave you all a fright but I'm fine.'

Dominic stared down at her upturned face, at the tear-stains and the shadows in her eyes as well as beneath and, with a sudden sigh, put his arms around her. The skipper's wife, the very soul of discretion, melted away up the ladder.

'Sure?' he said into her hair.

'Mmm...'

'You don't have to be *brave*.'

'I'm not,' she murmured. 'I think someone must have known how often this would happen to me and gave me good strong bones to compensate.' She lifted her head from his shoulder. 'You can go back if you like. You were enjoying it so much.'

His grey gaze was curiously sombre and his lips barely moved as he said, 'Stephanie, there are times when nothing about you makes sense at all. Do you—make sense to yourself?'

Any other time she might have found the right answer. But standing against him, with all his strength supporting her, all *her* responses and reactions thrown out of kilter as was her still trembling body, she could only say hopelessly, 'No...'

'There must be a key, some——'

'There isn't. It's a lost cause.' She looked at him despairingly. 'I've been trying to tell you that for so *long*...'

He closed his eyes briefly as fresh tears came to hers and held her closer. 'All right. This isn't the time or place for another encounter of our kind. Come upstairs—we're about an hour from Hayman. Let's see if we can't make it enjoyable for you too. Ever sailed a boat?'

Her lips parted in surprise. 'No! And I'm quite sure I'd be useless at it.'

He smiled unexpectedly. 'Not with me to teach you, Mrs Rayburn. Are you quite sure you haven't done yourself any damage?' He held her away from him and surveyed her from head to toe.

'Yes. Dominic, I don't know if this is a good idea...'

It was a surprisingly good idea and even Veronica, who was now in a winsome, captivating mood, exerted herself to make the last hour a pleasant one. So, as Stephanie stood at the wheel and took in some rudimentary sailing lessons good cheer was the order and with the wind in her hair, Dominic right behind her and somehow infusing composure to her battered body and spirits, she almost forgot her burdens.

It was also with a slightly bemused but glowing expression that she said as they docked, 'It's really quite simple, isn't it?'

Dominic grinned and the skipper forbore to comment at all on the subject but it was plain to see he was pleased her day had ended happily.

It was Dominic who took matters further in hand, somewhat upsetting Veronica's winsome mood, by declining an invitation for dinner with impeccable, charming grace and the simple statement that he thought Stephanie should take things easy.

Warwick was immediately understanding but he said, ignoring his wife's pout, 'Let's meet for an early business breakfast tomorrow, Dominic. Then we can spent the rest of the day entertaining the ladies. I'll give you a call.'

Stephanie felt Dominic go still for a moment before he assented readily, and she knew then that this was going to be the crucial meeting.

Back in their room, she said uncertainly, 'I'm really all right if you would have preferred to meet them tonight. He's going to get down to brass tacks tomorrow, isn't he? So if you think it would be diplomatic to have dinner with them——'

'No, I don't. Take your clothes off, Stephanie.'

She gasped and colour flooded her face.

'So that I can see for myself,' he said deliberately, 'just how fine you are. Did you think I was going to rape you?'

Her tongue tied itself in knots.

'You did,' he said dispassionately.

'No!' she got out at last.

'Seduce you, then.' He folded his arms. 'Or merely exercise my conjugal rights.' He lifted an eyebrow.

'You . . . you're impossible,' she said shakily. 'There's nothing wrong with me.'

'Then show me—otherwise I'll get the nurse. You may be used to tumbling about a bit, my beanpole wife, but that was a fair fall. And now the elation of sailing the boat has worn off, you look ready to collapse. If you won't do it, I will—and I might still get the nurse.'

'I...'

But he advanced towards her purposefully.

Some minutes later, when she was totally naked and shaking with anger at the way she'd been coolly and clinically inspected, he picked her up and carried her into the bathroom where he put her down, kept his arm about her waist and turned on the shower.

'Contrary to popular belief, a cool shower will help you most now,' he said placidly and, without further ado, lifted her again and put her under the stream of water.

Stephanie yelped but he spanned her waist with his hands and kept her there, getting quite wet himself in the process but apparently uncaring, and apparently unmoved by what the cold water was doing to her nipples and how it slicked down her long, slender thighs and small hips. Then he lifted her out and wrapped her in a towel.

'There.' He flicked her wet hair off her face. 'Now I'll order you a good stiff brandy.'

'I hate you,' she said through her teeth.

'At least I know you're not nursing something worse than a few...' he smiled faintly '...spectacular bruises. And I thought you'd prefer my bedside manner to be professional—rather than anything else.'

'Your bedside manner,' she said bitterly, 'is utterly brutal.'

He laughed. 'And you're looking more like your old self. Dinner in bed, a video if you'd like, then a good long sleep should complete the cure. I'll bring your nightgown in to you.'

'It's only six-thirty!' she protested. 'And why you feel I need to be modest now escapes me.'

A little glint lit his eyes. 'It could be for my protection, dear Stephanie. And who cares about the time? You were up at the crack of dawn.'

Two hours later they'd eaten in the room, Stephanie was in bed and Dominic had an array of papers spread out in front of him on the desk. The Patterson tender, she gathered.

She *was* feeling sleepy and grateful to be in bed but there was something mesmerising about him as he sat with his dark head bent, totally absorbed and with his gold pen flashing in the lamplight occasionally.

'Is something wrong?' she asked quietly at last.

He glanced up in surprise. 'I thought you were asleep. No. I'm just going over everything so it's all fresh in my mind and I don't have to keep consulting these.' He lifted a paper and let it flutter down.

'I suppose,' she said musingly, 'it will be quite something to get an order from America for your boats.'

'Quite something,' he agreed wryly. 'Actually, Mike had a lot to do with it. He designed this rather unique prototype that really caught Warwick's eye.'

'So,' she said slowly, 'this has been quite a family effort—how ironic.'

He was silent and she wished she could retract her words because she had no desire to breach the peace of the last two hours.

Then he said into the silence, 'You're not much alike for twins, are you?' He threw his pen down and leant back in the chair, flexing his shoulders.

'No, although we do have one thing in common...' She broke off.

'Tell me.'

She grimaced and pushed her arms behind her head. 'We share the same weakness; it's just taken different forms.'

'If you mean you go around taking what isn't yours...' He turned fully towards her with his eyes suddenly narrowed.

'Do I?' she whispered and put a hand over her eyes suddenly.

'Is that what you meant?' He sounded incredulous.

'I...no.' She took her hand away wearily. 'But it seemed to fit, didn't it?'

'What did you mean?'

'That we both have an awful chip on our shoulders.'

'That's not so surprising, I guess,' he said thoughtfully, 'but there's a whole lot more to you than there is to Mike, Stephanie. And one day you're going to tell me the truth about—us. Because until you do, we'll never really be free of each other.'

'I told you this morning——'

'You also told me couple of days ago that you'd never slept with anyone else. Is that true?' His voice was deep and quiet and although she willed herself not to look at him she couldn't resist the unspoken power that flowed from him and eventually crumbled her defences.

'Yes,' she said starkly, their gazes catching and clinging at last.

'Then there has to be another explanation for us.'

'But——'

'What you told me this morning doesn't make sense,' he said drily. 'Private revenge, a private feather in your cap—no.'

She licked her lips. 'It occurred to you at the time, Dominic.'

'I was working in the dark at the time. Now I'm working with half a script, you might say, but I know you much better and it just doesn't jell. But what does?'

He was speaking more to himself, she realised, and for a terrified moment held her breath, because of course there was only one other explanation, wasn't there? The one that had apparently never occurred to him.

He went on then, still more to himself, 'If I'm the first and only lover you've had——' his eyes focused on her suddenly '—were you on the rebound that night, Stephanie? Did you love someone you couldn't have and what I mistook for attraction was...a kind of don't-care despair? Did...' he paused and searched her eyes '...I take the place of someone you could never have in your arms but not your heart—and you've never forgiven yourself or me especially since you found out I can always arouse you physically?'

She stared at him, paralysed.

'Is that the nature of your conflict, Stephanie?' he said very quietly. 'Do you still think of him when you're in my arms, making love to me?'

She put a hand to her mouth helplessly because if you twisted what he'd said only a little there was so much fateful truth in it—he'd virtually guessed it all now excepting that it hadn't been *don't-care* despair and that *he* was the one she'd thought she could never have, and still believed it.

He stood up, came over to the bed and stared down at her and she could see that what he'd said was taking root in his mind as his eyes roamed her. Then he said with a curious mixture of gentleness and determination, 'I won't let you go until you tell me.'

'Dominic, you promised...'

'I made that promise in error, Stephanie. Look, I'm adult and not sinless myself. We're both adults and your life is going to be hell if you're going to go on wanting me and hating yourself for it. For your sake alone, why don't you at least try to share the burden with me? I might not be the stuff your dreams are made of but at least I know you better than most—I have to—and you could even find I understand better than most. Actually...' he touched her upturned, dazed and wary face '...sleep on it. I didn't mean to stir it all up again tonight. I'm going for a walk.'

CHAPTER SIX

IT WAS a long time before Stephanie moved after the door closed quietly behind Dominic.

Then she pulled a pillow into her arms and hugged it as she realised with a pang that she was exhausted and defeated. Perhaps the fall hadn't helped but something had finally severed her resistance to the truth and opened her eyes to the only possibility of releasing herself from the anguish of this marriage and, not only that, had opened her eyes to the fact that he deserved to know the truth—what little he still didn't know, she thought painfully.

The other truth—what he felt for her—well, there lay the crux of the matter as it always had. But if I'd been honest from the start I might not have got myself on to this awful treadmill, she reflected. If I'd buried my awful pride would I be any worse off than I am now?

She fell asleep with that thought going round and round in her head.

It was very early again when she woke to sunlight patterning the floor through the louvres but this time she wasn't alone. Dominic was stretched out beside her.

It was like a blow to her heart. He lay on his front with his arms pushed under the pillow, the sheet caught about his waist, and what he wore beneath it she couldn't tell but his long back was bare.

And the love in her heart spilled over, never to be denied again. It made no difference that he could and had been cruel and arrogant, no difference that he'd used her to further his business—he was right, from what he knew she'd used him first. Nothing made any difference to the fact that this was the man she yearned for and always had, yearned now to have him wake up and smile at her and make love to her but with the warmth and tenderness she knew could exist between two people.

She sighed and moved then tensed as he stirred but the damage was done. He rolled over and put out an arm sleepily and it encountered her thigh. In the moments before he opened his eyes, while his fingers lingered on her, she wondered with a sense of heartbreak if it was someone else he thought he was waking up to.

Then his eyes opened and he turned his head but even straight from sleep his grey gaze was inscrutable although he withdrew his hand almost immediately.

She took a breath and knew suddenly what she had to do, and knew that she'd have to gather every ounce of courage she possessed because, whether he believed her or not, she could no longer live this lie, and if he did believe her she had to withstand his pity.

She pushed a pillow up behind her so she was half sitting, staring straight ahead, and she swallowed twice and said, 'I'm ready to tell you the truth now.'

He moved abruptly and muttered something beneath his breath.

'I know...' her voice shook slightly '...that it's probably not the best time but I mightn't have the courage later. I did what I did that night, that first night, because I'd never got over the adolescent crush I had on you at school. When it first started,' she smiled painfully, 'I used to dream that it wasn't impossible, that you would notice me and,' she pulled the sheet up a bit higher, 'even after I fell off my bike and was so awkward and I couldn't help but realise that to you I must seem like an exceptionally gangly schoolgirl, I still didn't quite stop dreaming. That was the only reason I went to Melissa's party.'

She paused and pleated the sheet then smoothed it carefully. 'If we'd never met again, it might have been the best thing that ever happened to me. Not only because of what Melissa said but you yourself. I knew, after that night, that I was asking for the moon. So I set about trying to forget, trying to grow up and to an extent I even learnt to accept that I was a bit different. Boys, men, clothes just didn't mean much to me. I think I decided I was a plain person...no,' she said as he moved, 'not so much in looks—it's hard to explain but that I was a practical, down-to-earth type with only one passion in life—my painting.'

The room was quite silent until he said, 'Go on.'

'Then we met again and...' she bit her lip but forced herself to continue '...in just a matter of minutes I knew that I'd been kidding myself, that I'd been living with only half of me and there was a woman within me, a real woman that unfortunately...seemed only to respond to you. I just couldn't see how I could feel the same way about anyone else. I still don't know—yes, I do,' she corrected herself, 'I wasn't drunk. It was that I suddenly couldn't bear to be that kind of half-person any longer—even though I knew you weren't for me and never could be. I thought—I can go on alone then although it will probably always hurt but at least I'll be whole, not the sort of insulated, sexless creature I'd been before. I don't know if this is making any sense to you but...' She shrugged and touched the sheet to her eyes.

'And the next morning?' he said sombrely.

She sniffed and said huskily, 'The next morning? The next morning was a traditional morning after the night before. Nothing was so clear-cut any more. That was the first time you rendered me all dazed,' she said and tried to smile. 'I couldn't think straight, I didn't know what to do—I even wanted to cancel the trip but I didn't and what I did do was how I came a real cropper.' She told him quite simply how she'd seen him as she'd come out of the bank. 'And that's when I said to myself—all right, you knew this was going to hurt, you'd better start to live with it straight away. That's also when my pride took over... Perhaps I can only say in my defence that, while I knew and have known ever since in my heart of hearts what happened to me, I also knew I was still asking for the moon.'

'Stephanie, that girl was a school friend and yes, we had gone out together years before but she'd come to tell me she was getting married, that's why she was glowing and why I kissed her.'

Stephanie moved her shoulders. 'All the same, even if I'd known, I would have still felt the contrast. Let's—I've told you the truth, let's keep it honest. I know now, the way things have worked out, that I should have told you years ago. But *you* know how stiff-necked I am about charity. If you believe anything I've said, and you more or less said it all last night, if you feel anything for me, let me go now, Dominic. Please,' she whispered, then moved her hands. 'After this is over.'

'Oh, lord,' he said beneath his breath, then, 'Let's get one thing straight—you talked about asking for the moon. That doesn't come into it at all if you mean what I think you mean—that you're not good enough for me. You don't really believe that?' He sat up with a frown and pushed a hand through his hair. 'That's crazy.'

'No,' she said slowly, 'although, yes, at one stage I did but because I saw myself as *dull* and capable and—so different from the girl in red. But I was young and confused then.' She gestured helplessly. 'But when I say it now, what I mean is that I can't help but know I'm not the woman who will...' She stopped and tried again. 'I think one knows one is in love when no one else will do for you and when the depths can't be deeper and the heights greater. I'm not that person for you although you want me sometimes. If I were...' She shrugged and reached for the sheet to pat her eyes again. 'It would be kinder not to lie to me, Dominic.'

He stared down at her for a long time then he took her hand and lay back, and he said with a weariness that took her breath away, 'What if there are never the real depths or heights for me?'

'Dominic?' she whispered.

'What if I really am one of those spiritually stunted sort of people? You thought you were, after all. Perhaps I'm the real thing. Real?' His lips twisted ironically. 'Not the right choice of words perhaps but you might know what I mean.'

Stephanie stared into his eyes with her lips parted. 'How long have you felt like this?' she queried huskily, her eyes dark and incredulous.

'Years,' he said drily. 'In fact my beloved grandmother, the same one who left the awkward will, saw it coming even before I did. She blamed my parents, said they spoilt me—and Melissa. She said everything came too easily: money, freedom, girls... She often used to say to me, "By the time you're thirty, Dominic Rayburn, you'll be cynical and disillusioned because all your God-given talents will have been wasted." She meant that I'd never had to strive for anything—that isn't quite true, as it happened. I certainly had to strive to get Rayburn's back on its feet—still am, although I don't envisage failing—but you'd have to be the first person to agree that I'm cynical and disillusioned... You might find what else she said to me amusing. She used to say, "It will be a good woman who will be the making of you, Dominic, and it takes more than looks, wealth and knowing how to please women to get yourself a really good one."'

Stephanie closed her eyes. 'I had no idea,' she whispered.

'Now you have, would you consider changing your mind and staying with me?'

Her lashes flew up and she made a protesting little sound.

'I don't mean what we've had before. I mean a real commitment this time.'

'No—even if your grandmother was *right*, she didn't discount the possibility of the right woman coming along for you.'

'Stephanie...' his grip tightened on her hand '...do you know *why* I married you? Not because it was expedient or because there were times when it didn't seem to matter who the hell I married but because you were so different from all the women I knew. The only one who'd ever walked away from me. The only one who'd made love to me with no pretence, no flattery, no frills, no...I've never been able to find the right words to describe that night and since we did marry I've been as faithful to you as you've been to me, although I can't deny I've thought of not being so faithful to you. But I never was and you're the one I kept coming back to. Don't you think that might mean you *are* the right one?'

'But...' Stephanie trembled.

'Oh, hell,' he said softly and rolled over swiftly to take her in his arms. 'If there's one thing I'd give heaven and earth to be able to say now, it would be that I'm not like this——'

'Don't,' she whispered. 'I wouldn't believe you and I'd far rather we kept on being honest with each other but I couldn't...' She stopped abruptly. Couldn't I? she wondered. How *could* I...?

The phone rang.

Dominic ignored it. 'Tell me what you're thinking.'

'I...'

It rang again. He swore. 'That'll be Warwick.' He squinted at his watch. 'Must be some peculiar transatlantic custom, breakfast and business.'

'You must go,' Stephanie said.

'No——'

'Yes, please.' Her voice was a little shaky. 'I need time to think.'

'This could take hours,' he said curtly and reached for the phone.

'No, Dominic,' she put her hand on his arm, 'you *must* go and, anyway, I need to be alone for a while. I'm all right, though. In a way I feel better about myself than I have for years but I need to get used to this—I won't do anything rash. I mean I'll be here to tell you whatever I decide.'

Before he left, he insisted on ordering her breakfast in bed, which she ate slowly, alone, and with her mind curiously blank. Eventually she had a shower, slipped into shorts and a blouse and decided that a walk might get her thought processes going.

It was a beautiful morning and the gardens of Hayman were drowsing in the sunlight and quite soon she became absorbed as she wandered through them. Who would not in the fragrant wonderland of gardenias and azaleas, star jasmine, portwine magnolia, agapanthus and clivia as well as the more tropical varieties such as bougainvillaea and poinciana, banana trees and spider lilies?

Then she came upon the Japanese garden and the perfection of it was breathtaking—more azaleas and magnolia but also black and heavenly bamboo, sago palms and lychee trees and a little wooden teahouse. For an age, all she could do was try to commit it all to memory not only as an artist but also because of the peace and tranquillity.

It was beside the pool and on the lawn beneath the date palms that lined the main entrance that she sank on to a stone bench and at last thought, Why does it help to know that he's disillusioned and disenchanted? That I'm the one he keeps coming back to—how can it give me hope? He can't stay this way forever and then I would have to let him go. What is this mystery that makes him the only man for me, and makes me care so greatly that I long to give him some solace and even subject myself to living with a Sword of Damocles hanging over me all the time? I don't know what to do—I am already married to him . . .

It was a bird in one of the palms that brought her out of her reverie, a black and white kurrawong, singing to the sky as if its life depended on it and then Dominic, coming down the path towards her, his dark hair ruffled, his hands shoved in his pockets—a more complex man than she'd realised and one with his own torments.

He stopped in front of her and they stared into each other's eyes for a long time, until she said, 'I would still go away and paint. I mean, sometimes I go into another world and I'm difficult to live with. I'm also . . .' she smiled shakily ' . . . not really a glitzy sort of person although I'd try not to embarrass you.'

He sat down beside her and put his arm around her and she hid her face in his shoulder for a long moment then looked up at him and saw the pain in his eyes, and felt herself calming.

'Just one thing,' she said huskily. 'Don't ever feel sorry for me, will you? That's the one thing I couldn't stand—and I promise I won't ever feel sorry for myself.' She put up a hand and touched his face gently. 'I think you'd better take me away and make love to me the way you wanted to the other night.'

It reminded her of that first night so long ago, the way he made love to her. The way her body seemed to come as a revelation to him again, so slender yet with some surprises, pale perfect breasts and nipples that were generous and velvety and sensitive even to his gaze upon them, nearly translucent delicate skin that bruised easily and was bruised.

'It has been too long,' he murmured as they lay facing each other. 'Far too long. No wonder I've been more bloody-minded than usual. Do you really—want this?'

They weren't touching and as she lay with her hair spread out on the pillow, waiting, she thought that again it was like that first night—the same restraint but less easy to understand now. 'Don't you? Has something changed?'

'No, nothing's changed.' He lifted his hand at last to cup her cheek and stared down into the greeny depths of her eyes. 'It's just that I probably don't deserve you.'

She smiled faintly. 'Who knows what they deserve?'

'But I've tormented you and mocked you and sometimes never more so than in bed, like this . . .'

'I did my share of mocking,' she whispered, and with a little sigh moved into his arms. 'Hold me,

please. I seem to need it rather desperately—perhaps
we both do.'

'Oh, God,' he said with an effort into her hair,
pulling her against the length of him, holding her
hard, and then he was laughing a little and she tilted
her head back to see his eyes. 'I didn't know where
to begin,' he said incredulously, letting her go a bit
and moving his hands up and down her back and
hips with his old sureness of touch. 'The weight of
my sins must have——'

'Shhh . . .'

'I must——'

'No, you mustn't. It's all behind us now.' But she
was laughing herself with secret relief yet joy as
well because he'd spoken from the heart.

They lay together then, in more mental unity than
they'd ever shared, touching, talking infrequently
and inconsequently as lovers—as they never had—
until they fell silent and his hands on her body no
longer sought to soothe but were moving on her
compellingly and more and more intimately,
stroking her nipples until they stood erect and she
shuddered; pursuing her trembling delight to its core
with the lightest touch so that there was only one
course on earth for her then. To welcome him, to
yearn for his weight on her, his thrust into her, to
open her heart and body to him alone. To be consumed by his strength and feel the smooth power
of his shoulders beneath her hands, to be guided
down the paths of passion the way, for her, it was
unthinkable anyone else should guide her.

Sometimes he lingered to inflict different delights on different areas of her arching, vibrant,
quivering body then he would re-establish the

rhythm as she too stroked and caressed and they kissed deeply. Until her small, husky sighs reached a crescendo and her hands were kneading and pleading and then, unerringly, he wrapped her hard in his arms as the final pleasure began to swamp them.

'It's no wonder,' she said, much later, 'that I don't know what to do with myself after you've finished with me.'

He laughed softly and kissed her hair. 'All right?'

'Yes—well, I don't know what time it is, I'm not even sure what day it is but otherwise I'm fine. Are you?'

He said wryly, 'Like you, I'm a bit dazed. Don't go away.'

'I'm not, I'm just pulling up the sheet.' She lay back and covered them both.

'Cold?' he said gravely but with a glint in his eye.

'No. Tired.' She laid her head on his chest. 'When do we have to meet the Pattersons?'

'Not until much later.'

'Thank heavens,' she whispered.

He smoothed her hair. 'You might say I've scored twice today.'

'Oh?'

'Yes. Warwick ordered his boats.'

Stephanie moved her cheek. 'Congratulations. Does...?' She broke off.

'Say it.'

'No, nothing.'

'Stephanie,' he said deliberately, 'in the light of this—us, believe me, that pales into insignificance.'

She hesitated, blinked away a tear then said simply, 'Thanks.'

They didn't leave their room until about four o'clock, then they wandered hand in hand down to the beach where the Pattersons were ensconced. The tide was in and there was just enough balmy breeze for all but one of the catamarans to be skimming the sunlit water between Hayman and Bali Ha'i— not the real Bali Ha'i but a small gem of an island towards Hook. Before they reached Warwick and Veronica they stopped to watch the Air Whitsunday flying boat take off and head for the mainland, Stephanie holding her breath unconsciously.

'From your expression,' he said with a grin, 'that wouldn't be one of your favourite modes of flight.'

'No—I'd be petrified,' she agreed and added ruefully, 'I didn't know my expressions were so revealing.'

'They might not be to others but they are to me.' He smiled into her eyes, causing her to feel weak with love, and kissed her parted lips lightly. 'Ready?'

She grimaced. 'As I'll ever be.'

'You've very quiet, Stephanie,' Veronica said wearily and petulantly about half an hour later.

'Sorry.' Stephanie stirred on her lounger. 'I was enjoying the view.' Now, that's a lie, she thought with a corner of her mouth quirking. I was actually remembering being made love to in every little detail and yes, I have to confess it, feeling like a cat who stole the cream. Because somehow or other you know what Dominic and I have been doing, don't you, Veronica? Your ESP has caught all the vibrations and it's driving you mad... Oh, dear, now who's being a bitch?

She was still feeling a bit guilty when Dominic said lazily that such sloth was sending him to sleep and he thought he'd take a 'cat' out. Veronica, quick as a flash, leapt up and demanded to be taken with him.

Dominic hesitated, his eyes inscrutable, then he said rather abruptly, 'Do you know anything about sailing?'

'Nothing,' Warwick said drily.

'Neither did Stephanie yesterday,' Veronica pointed out. 'Oh, come on—it's my turn today. Pretty please!'

He turned away with a shrug whereupon Veronica sauntered after him, the cynosure of all eyes in her tiny gold bikini, and when she caught up with him she put her arm through his and somehow managed to give the impression of being on secret, intimate terms with him.

They watched in silence, Stephanie and Warwick, as she balked at having to wear a life-jacket then made a great play of finding one that fitted. Then there seemed to be no way she could get aboard in the thigh-deep water without Dominic picking her up and putting her on. Finally, they got going.

That was when Warwick sighed and said tiredly, 'I must apologise for my wife, Stephanie.'

Stephanie bit her lip and, to her surprise, reached out a hand and laid it briefly on his. 'Please don't. We all... have our problems.'

'You're very understanding where many women wouldn't have been,' he said quietly. 'What I can't understand is how I could...do this to the memory of my first wife whom I loved deeply and who gave me an almost perfect daughter in her image.'

'Perhaps,' Stephanie said slowly, '*she* would understand how lonely you are without her.'

Warwick closed his eyes and was silent for a long time.

Until Stephanie said gently, 'Tell me about your daughter.'

'She...' Some of the tension drained from his face. 'She's twenty, she's nearly finished college, she's not very tall but she's got a good figure and the most enchanting oval face, shiny long brown hair, great dark eyes that laugh at you sometimes—she's a darling,' he said proudly. 'She's also pretty sensible—she doesn't seem to be hell-bent on living with some guy yet although there are plenty of beaus about. You two'd like each other; you could even be kindred spirits—she's studying art. Yes, I reckon two of a kind, sensible girls but...' he grinned as Stephanie looked wry '...honeys all the same...'

'Thank—— What is it?' she asked, following his suddenly narrowed gaze.

Warwick sat up. 'They've capsized!'

'I'm sure if anyone can handle that Dominic can.'

Famous last words, she was to realise shortly, because the cat refused to be righted, apparently, and the rescue dinghy set out from the beach with a roar.

What followed was really very comic, unless you were aware of the tensions below the surface. Dominic got into the dinghy with no trouble at all but Veronica had to be hauled aboard most inelegantly and one of the two crew members, a girl, swam to the cat, flipped it upright with no trouble at all, and was left to sail it in.

So it was a bedraggled, dishevelled Veronica who climbed out of the dinghy when it reached shore, spurning Dominic's help this time and making it quite plain to all within earshot that she was in a towering temper...

'He didn't...he wouldn't,' Stephanie whispered disbelievingly as Veronica's extremely colourful tirade rang out.

'You did!'

Stephanie stared incredulously at her husband some time later in the privacy of their room. She had returned there alone when it had become obvious that the idyllic afternoon had been shattered. Veronica, further to her ire, had been commanded to go to hers by *her* husband in such freezing, disgusted tones that she'd flounced off furiously and Stephanie had taken the opportunity to melt away, leaving the two men facing each other, both looking particularly grim.

Which Dominic still was as he came in.

'You deliberately capsized her, gave her an awful fright and nearly drowned her,' Stephanie accused, repeating the repeatable part of what Veronica had said.

'She deserved it—the stupid bitch,' he answered coldly. 'If you'd heard the proposition she put to me you might not be siding with her! But she was in no danger—we were only in about four feet of water and she didn't even get that much of a fright—she was more worried about her bloody hair getting wet.'

'I'm not...' Stephanie sat down on the bed and discovered her shoulders were shaking—with laughter. 'Oh, Dominic,' she said at last, tears running down her cheeks, 'someone should have warned her about you. But...' She sobered. 'Warwick...is he all right?'

'I offered to tear up the contract,' Dominic said moodily. 'I said it was an unforgivable thing to have done to have embarrassed them both like that and I'd understand if he didn't want to have anything further to do with me. He refused. And now I feel like a real heel!' He threw his towel away from him.

'What else did he say?'

'That it was her behaviour that had embarrassed him but that was his problem and it had nothing to do with business. That they would be leaving this afternoon if possible—and could I pass a message on to you.'

Stephanie tensed.

'He said to tell you he'd decided his memories were more precious to him than anything else.' He raised an eyebrow at her.

'He mentioned his first wife to me while you were sailing. He also apologised for Veronica and told me about his daughter. I think...' she put her hands to her cheeks anxiously '...he means to leave her.'

Dominic sat down beside her and put an arm around her shoulders. 'And so he should,' he said quietly. 'Which is not to say I don't feel as guilty as hell at the moment and I'd far rather he'd had no encouragement from me but there are some things you shouldn't subject yourself to and a marriage like that is one of them.'

They sat in silence for a while until he lifted her on to his lap and leant back with her. 'Talking of marriages,' he said, moving his chin on her hair and cradling her in his arms, 'how is this one doing at the moment? By the way, I'm probably the last one to be sermonising.'

'This one?' She fiddled with his watch band. 'I have to say, although I probably shouldn't—it's not a very worthy thought—I think it's received quite a boost. At poor Veronica's expense—I was only thinking earlier that I can also be a bitch,' she added with a little laugh and suddenly pink cheeks.

'What made you think that?' He bent his head and his lips twitched as he saw her rueful, flushed expression.

'Well, this afternoon when I was so quiet it wasn't because of the view. I was dreaming about something and feeling positively smug.'

'Dreaming about us,' he hazarded with a gleam of pure devilry in his eyes.

'Something like that.' She shrugged.

'May I take it, then, despite all the trauma we've had today...' he grimaced ' ... one way or another, that you still approve of "us"?'

'So far, certainly,' she replied but as she looked into his eyes it was a more revealing glance than she realised. It held her sudden confusion, her perhaps unconscious disbelief that things could be this way between them, and held her vulnerability that was perhaps even greater now that he knew her true feelings.

'Stephanie,' he said very quietly, 'don't look like that—do you know why I did what I did this afternoon? Why I really dunked Veronica? Not only because she was desperate to cheat on her marriage and make a fool of a man who didn't deserve it, but because the contrast between the two of you was suddenly so great. She really thought she was irresistible—even when I was searching for the key to unlock your mind and I was bitter and angry with you, I never mistook you for the shallow, selfish person she is, someone who thinks she's all woman but is only a mockery of the real thing. That's what made me do it. You.'

'If that's a compliment...' She wiped her eyes with the back of her hand.

'It is.' He kissed her wet lashes.

'Thank you—but now I feel guilty too.'

'Don't. It was bound to happen sooner or later. Should we—drown our guilt together?' A new note entered his voice.

'What do you have in mind?'

'That marble bath is big enough for both of us. Why don't we share it, then dress up and find ourselves a mouth-watering meal—and bring a bottle of champagne back to share? In bed.'

She stared up at him gravely. 'That sounds positively decadent.' Her lips curved. 'But also deliciously so,' she added demurely.

CHAPTER SEVEN

'WHAT can I say to your mother?' Stephanie said worriedly a week later as they flew home from Hayman. 'Not to mention your sister.'

Dominic grinned. 'Leave Melissa to me, but my mother's a very amiable person.'

Stephanie raised an eyebrow, which he noted. 'You find that hard to believe?' he queried seriously.

'Rather.'

'You assumed all we Rayburns were made in the same mould?'

'It did occur to me,' she said thoughtfully.

'Then I have a surprise for you—we'll go and see her as soon as we arrive. Happy?'

Stephanie turned her head to him on the seat-back and the way his grey eyes searched hers, the knowledge in them of the way she was, brought some colour to her cheeks. 'Don't you know?' she said huskily.

He put his hand over hers. 'Tell me.'

She lowered her lashes. 'I hardly know where I am or what day it is. I'll . . . have to get over it soon otherwise, well, it's not a good way to be.'

His fingers slid through hers. 'I think it's a very good way to be, for a wife. I can certainly recommend it, as a husband.'

Her lips curved into a faint smile. 'I'm sure wives should have some more practical qualities too. The honeymoon can't last forever, can it? So I'll set about trying shortly——'

'Look at me, Stephanie,' he said on a different note and she looked up with a sudden frown. 'Contrary to what you obviously believe, the way you are when we make love, the way you are now, means more than all the practicalities in the world. Remember that. I just wish I could show you.'

'Well, you can't,' she said a little breathlessly and he laughed quietly at the way she looked around anxiously.

'I can in thought,' he murmured. 'Isn't that supposed to be the same thing?' Her hand trembled beneath his, causing him to raise a wicked eyebrow. 'I never believed that, actually, but perhaps there's more to it than I thought.'

'You're impossible, Dominic,' she said wryly. 'We're nearly there.'

'Saved by the bell,' he drawled as the stewardess went past on her final inspection of seatbelts, but he didn't release her hand.

They didn't say much as they landed but, for some reason she couldn't establish, Stephanie found herself turning the conversation over in her mind as they took a taxi to his mother's flat. Then the reality of coming face to face with Mrs Rayburn Senior, who, despite what Dominic thought, could quite reasonably be expected to have a whole range of bitter emotions at her command on the subject of her errant daughter-in-law, wiped it from her mind.

But he was right again. His mother stared at him, at Stephanie's hand in his, critically then fully at her with a dawning of surprise in her eyes.

Stephanie tensed but Mrs Rayburn really astonished her. She said, admittedly in well-bred exasperated tones but all the same she said it, 'I can't pretend to understand any of this—I never did, but welcome to the family, my dear. If you must know I've been dying to meet you and talk to you but Dominic warned me off and unfortunately he's very like his father in that respect. What he says goes...either that or I haven't got very much backbone! Perhaps the simplest thing I can say is— I'm so pleased you two have decided to be happy together; it really is the best way. Oh, dear! Am I going to cry?' And she advanced on them with her hands outstretched.

'You were right about your mother,' Stephanie said, in another taxi. 'I liked her.'

'So do I. You were right too.' He looked at her wryly.

'What do you mean?'

'How she survived the battering she received from us all I don't know. My father, his mother, Melissa, me—Rayburns all and all either autocratic or tempestuous or both, and all with a tendency to be bloody-minded.'

'Yes, well...' Stephanie smiled faintly '...but I haven't ousted her from her home, have I?'

'No, she made that decision when my father died. She said it was very tempting to languish there with her memories but she thought she should set about making a new life although she did insist it should stay in the family for future generations. Melissa had already found her own place so it was left to me to stay on. Here we are.'

Stephanie stared at the house in the late afternoon sunlight as they rode up the drive and felt her nerves prickle. She said slowly, 'It's a lovely old house—and garden.'

He frowned suddenly. 'I hope you're not going to associate it with any...old memories.'

'Would that be stupid, do you think?'

He didn't answer immediately but concentrated on paying off the driver and getting their luggage out of the boot. And it was only when they were alone in the middle of the drive that he said firmly, 'Yes, Stephanie.'

Easy for you to say, she thought, but she said, 'Right. Anyway, were you to carry out a time-honoured practice, that might superimpose new and more powerful memories.'

'Ah. I think I know what you mean. Step this way, ma'am.' He led her up the steps, unlocked the front door then swung her into his arms and over the threshold. 'Did I get it right?' he queried, walking along the passage and pushing open another door with his foot.

'Absolutely, but——' She stopped as he laid her down on a double bed.

'This is the master bedroom,' he said gravely and removed his jacket and shirt.

'Oh. Dominic—right now?' She sat up and pushed her hair off her face. It had come out of its ribbon.

'Definitely; when you're in the master bedroom, what the master says goes.' He sat down beside her and took her in his arms.

'You should have warned me,' she murmured as he started to unbutton her blouse.

'Now you know.' He slipped his hands behind her and unhooked her bra. 'Any objections?'

'Well, our luggage is still sitting in the middle of the drive and ... Dominic ...' Her voice sank as he cupped her breasts and looked down at them, so pale and vulnerable against the tanned strength of his hands.

'As for the mistress of the house, didn't we decide on her main role earlier?' he said, looking up at last.

'You decided,' she said raggedly.

'That's not only because I'm wise in these matters, Stephanie,' he said with an entirely wicked kind of sobriety, 'but also desperate. Could you see your way clear to humour me in this all else aside, do you think?'

She stared into his eyes, noted the teasing little glint as well as the desire, but it didn't stop her from going weak with love and her own hunger. She didn't have to say anything after that.

But later, as she lay drowsily on the double bed in the master bedroom listening to Dominic taking a shower, she found herself thinking back to their conversation on the plane and again wondered why, and wondered why even the intensity of his love-making had not quite blocked out the sort of wariness this house seemed to arouse in her. And she discovered that she'd have preferred to start out their reborn marriage in a place with no memories. But she immediately told herself not to be foolish; that was no way to make this commitment work, to be clinging to old memories, although was there something else she couldn't put her finger on? It was a little while, in fact, before she did put her finger on it.

Dominic took a few more days off work and took her up to see Nan the next day, who expressed very similar sentiments to Mrs Rayburn, and when Stephanie apologised for deserting her so abruptly she said she'd been thinking of taking an extended trip around Australia for some time.

Dominic expressed some surprise at Stephanie's possessions as they packed them into his car. 'Is this the lot?' In fact there were more canvasses than anything else.

'Yes.'

'You travel light—through life,' he said slowly.

Stephanie shrugged. 'As a family we didn't gather many possessions, only the essentials.'

He frowned but when she asked him what was wrong he said nothing and didn't allude to it again.

A few nights later Melissa descended on them, in typical Melissa fashion.

'So,' she said, taking off her exquisite leather jacket and handing it to Stephanie, 'it's all to be out in the open now! You look different, Stephanie.'

Stephanie glanced down at one of her new outfits and conceded that she did.

'Dom's doing, no doubt.' Melissa accepted a drink from her brother and raised her thin, pencilled brows at him. 'What, may I ask, wrought this miracle? And are you seeking my approval?'

'Not at all,' Dominic said pleasantly. 'Nor need you exert yourself trying to fathom it all out.'

Melissa's mouth tightened. 'I see. Well——' But she broke off, perhaps because of a warning glint in her brother's eyes, and she visibly backed down during the hour she spent with them although she declined an invitation to stay to dinner.

After she had left, Stephanie stood in the middle of the lounge, staring at nothing absently.

Dominic came up behind her and put his hands on her shoulders, massaging them gently.

'Nothing's changed there,' Stephanie said after a while, leaning back against him.

'No. But the ice is broken. Melissa...' he paused '...has her own demons.'

'Yes. I guess we all have those.'

The next morning Stephanie was alone in the house for the first time and suddenly very conscious that this was a new life that was going to require a lot of adjustments, more for her than for Dominic, because he was very much on his home ground if nothing else.

And the feeling got stronger as she wandered round the house and tried to convince herself she was now mistress of it. Not only that but a mistress of substance with a cleaning lady who came in twice a week and her own car—Dominic had handed her the keys of the second car in the garage and told her it was hers now. But, instead of being filled with wifely zeal, she felt lonely and disorientated, she discovered, and had to take herself severely to task. In the end what soothed her and kept a curious little streak of panic at bay was choosing one of the spare rooms and setting it up as a studio.

It was her painting, and the gardens of Hayman fresh in her mind, that helped considerably over those first weeks, together with her own garden. The inhibitions she suffered over the house didn't appear to extend to the garden, which, while always tidy from the ministrations of a gardening firm, lacked tender loving care—so she said to Dominic.

'It does?' He raised an eyebrow at her.

'Definitely.'

'That could be a problem.'

'Oh, I wouldn't mind doing it,' she assured him. 'I always dreamt of having the time to make a marvellous garden and I love painting flowers and trees—Nan has a fabulous garden but she was rather exclusive about it. She didn't really like anyone reconnoitering with her roses or pandering to her petunias,' she added gravely.

'Now that,' he drawled, 'is what I mean.'

'I don't get it.'

'If you intend to be reconnoitering with or pandering to anyone, it should be me.'

Stephanie stared at him expressionlessly then she said innocently, 'I don't think I know how to reconnoitre.'

'Oh, I think you do,' he said softly. It was a Sunday morning and they were sitting on the back step in the sunshine, drinking coffee.

'Well...' She considered and watched his hand on her thigh then she said demurely, 'I might be in the hands of an expert. Perhaps I have picked up a few little tips on the way.'

'Just a few?'

'Just a few...your mother is coming to lunch in about forty-five minutes, Dominic.'

'My mother, as I've told you, is a very good-natured woman.'

'If we have to rush, though, who knows what might happen? On the other hand, if we made a date for when she's gone we could . . . do it in style.'

His hand stilled on her thigh. 'Now that—is an offer I can't refuse but in the meantime I shall have to do something to cool my ardour. Come and show me where I can dig you a garden bed or cut down a tree—you're laughing,' he accused.

'Yes,' she giggled. 'Because you're teasing me.'

'If you really think that,' he said wryly, 'you aren't as experienced a reconnoiterer as I thought.'

'That's what I was trying to tell you!' She wriggled away, still laughing, and fled into the house.

Thus her love-affair with the garden, as Dominic called it, began. If he noticed that it didn't extend to the house, he made no comment.

In fact she'd just made the decision that he was amazingly easy to live with, and was starting to feel less tense about this new life, when he demonstrated some of his old arrogance in a way that hurt her and also brought back the sense of unease she'd not been able to explain to herself—but this time an explanation did occur to her.

It all blew up so quickly. He was very late home one evening and, as it happened, although she was inspired to paint, she'd torn herself away from the canvas and cooked a complicated dinner, only to have to sit and watch it dry out as the evening went past with no word from him.

To her dismay, she found herself wondering where he was and who he was with, then she was just beginning to worry that he'd had an accident when he walked in, kissed her absently, eyed her burnt offering and said he'd eaten.

Stephanie closed the oven door carefully. 'You could have let me know.'

He shrugged and pulled some sketches out of his briefcase. 'Sorry.' He didn't attempt to explain where he'd been.

Stephanie trembled. 'No, you're not!' And she picked up the dish of what should have been rare roast beef and crisp roast potatoes and deposited the lot, dish as well, in the rubbish bin.

Dominic's grey eyes narrowed but he said nothing so she then consigned the cauliflower *au gratin* and the honeyed carrots, the fresh fruit salad and cream into the bin with some force.

'Stephanie,' he said coldly then, 'aren't you being a little ridiculous?'

'Am I? It doesn't feel ridiculous. I spent quite some time doing it all when I could have been doing something else so what actually seems ridiculous to me is that you didn't even have the common courtesy to let me know you wouldn't be home!'

'My dear,' he drawled, 'doesn't it *also* seem to you that we're having an incredibly trite, tired old row that I could understand if you were a badly educated, hidebound shrew——'

Stephanie picked up a pot of mustard and threw it at him. It missed and he came round the table and caught her wrist in an iron grip. 'Now, look here,' he said grimly, 'I've got a business to run and all this—your home, your studio, your car, your *garden*—depend on how well I run it and the last thing I need is to be constantly worried about whether I'm infringing *your* ridiculous timetables.

If you'd wanted a lap-dog type of husband you could tyrannise and the kind of ultra-conventional marriage that revolves around domestic routine—which comes as a surprise from you, dear Stephanie,' he said sardonically, 'you're in the wrong house.'

Both what he said and the way he said it with that mocking glitter in his eyes which she knew so well of old rendered her speechless for a few moments, and it was worse because nothing about him since they'd started to live together had prepared her for this callous attack. Then words formed and she spoke them through her teeth.

'What we're talking about, Dominic, has nothing to do with ultra-conventional marriages or the fact that I should crawl to you because of all the things you're providing me with—if that's not an ultra-conventional, hidebound, utterly chauvinistic view of marriage I don't know what is—but to do with simple good manners. Take your hands *off* me because I'm about to leave *your* house which reeks, incidentally, with the possible exception of your mother, of all your arrogant, bloody-minded family of which you would have to take the prize for being the most objectionable!'

He released her wrist and stepped back. 'Right,' he said unpleasantly. 'Got a taxi fare on you again? Is that why you travel so lightly through life, Stephanie—so you can always just up stakes when the going gets a bit rough?'

Stephanie ground her teeth then stormed out of the back door, slamming it behind her.

But even the scented stillness of the garden failed to soothe her and she marched back in presently and into the master bedroom to find him already in bed but not asleep. To add insult to injury, he was reading more papers from his briefcase and he continued to read for several moments before he lifted his eyes to hers.

Then he put them down, stretched—he was naked to the waist—and said with the kind of lazy menace of a black puma biding its time with its prey firmly in its sights, 'If you find me so objectionable, I'm surprised you still care to come to bed with me.'

'I'm not coming to bed with you,' she retorted and removed her nightgown from beneath her pillow with jerky, angry movements. 'There are four other beds in this house, of which I shall make a choice. But if you were anything but an arrogant bastard, *you* would offer to sleep in a spare bed.'

'More etiquette, dear Stephanie?' he mocked. 'I'm afraid you're wasting your time. My gentlemanly instincts must not be very well developed because I'm damned if I'm sleeping in any spare room. Neither, for that matter...' he sat up in one lithe movement and caught her wrist '... are you.'

She collapsed on to the bed in a heap with an angry gasp. 'So if,' he continued, smiling coolly down at her flushed face and furious eyes, at her tangled legs where her skirt had ridden up and the way her blouse was moving in and out, 'you still want to fight me, it will have to be here.'

'The last thing I want to do is fight you,' she said contemptuously and added for good measure because she could see what was in his eyes despite the mockery, 'And don't try to make love to me, don't you dare! I'm not in the mood for it.'

'Got a sudden headache?' he queried contemptuously. 'That's another good old hidebound——'

'Well, I *have*,' she spat at him. 'At least something in my head is suffering from a curious aversion to you but let's call it a headache, it's the same thing.'

He let her wrist go abruptly but before she had time to gather herself he bent over and took her into his arms, saying curtly, 'Listen, I'm not prepared to drag this out with cold silences and nights in the spare room and what I'm trying to say is this: I can't be pinned down with these kind of tantrums and if,' he said significantly, 'you're already imagining all sorts of rubbish such as you imagined when you saw me kissing a girl in a red outfit then we haven't much chance of making this marriage work at all.'

The way she bit her lip gave her away but, beyond a sudden hardening of his mouth, he didn't pursue it. He said, 'So, if you'd wanted to paint, you should have gone ahead, if you'd really wanted to make a special dinner all you had to do was give me a ring and find out if it was a good night for it, but I'm sorry if you resent this house because there's nothing I intend to do about that—other than point out to you that it's rather childish in my estimation. Now, we could make love or we could go to sleep. I'm in favour of the former but I shall bow to your preference.'

She stared up into his eyes and shivered inwardly because despite his last words there was still an implacability about him and a warning in his eyes, and she knew there was a barrier between them she couldn't hope to cross over even if she were to try belatedly to reason with him. So what could she do—retreat with as much grace as she could muster and perhaps regret not having tried a more reasonable line in the first place? But why do I always have to be the reasonable one, the one who adjusts...?

She closed her eyes briefly then said, although she couldn't help the slightly dry tone in her voice, 'They do say that you should never let the sun go down on a quarrel. Well, you know what I mean.'

'I do. Is that an invitation to...? I mean I wouldn't dream of going so far as to make love to you without your permission,' he said gravely.

'Wouldn't you?' She smiled faintly and blinked away a foolish tear at the same time. 'You appear to be undressing me without my permission.'

He didn't stop and finally drew her under the sheets. Without her nightgown. 'I'm oddly addicted to undressing you, Stephanie,' he remarked. 'I can't seem to help myself.' And he slid his fingers into her hair and started to kiss her.

The next morning, the row might not have occurred. He was perfectly normal and so was she—until she was alone in the house again. Then she made herself a cup of coffee and took it into her studio but the urge to paint had left her and she stared at the canvas in a brown study for a long time. Because in the light of sober reflection she didn't think she had been so unreasonable last night, although she did acknowledge with a grimace that trite old rows were only trite because they were so true. But she also felt as if her not too unnatural rebellion had been crushed by a Panzer division of tanks. As if there'd been an implicit warning in it that had to do not solely with his work but his whole life—that's it, she thought with a pang. That's what I've been trying to pin down. He wants me, I can't doubt that, but as a mistress and not really an integral part of his life yet; it's still his life, not *ours*, in which I only have one primary role... And last night was a thinly veiled warning not to try to take over his life as he saw it. It had to be.

She sighed desolately and reminded herself that she'd always known this reborn marriage couldn't be perfect, that she'd have to tread carefully—how had she lost sight of it? How could she always be on guard—did she have any choice?

'No,' she whispered. 'I made the decision, I suppose mostly in the hope that one day he would love me as I love him; I'll just have to go on trying and hoping.'

Over the next weeks she succeeded mostly but it was hard to still—now that she'd acknowledged it—the feeling that she was a wife in name but a mistress in reality. And their lifestyle contributed to it. He didn't seem interested in entertaining or being entertained; he *was* working very hard, she knew, on a diversification into a new type of boat and she couldn't deny that she provided his rest and relaxation—times that she also couldn't deny gave her hope and encouragement—but how she filled the rest of *her* days didn't seem to occur to him so long as she was there for him. Not that she would normally fill them any differently, she reflected drily once. His mother had not only dutifully but genuinely tried to include her in her circle of friends and their daughters but that meant rounds of luncheons, games of golf and frequent shopping trips and visits to the hairdresser. Not me and never was, Stephanie had tried to explain without hurting Mrs Rayburn's feelings and then recently found herself wanting to shout that she felt like a fraud anyway because they *were* all wives while she felt like an impostor.

She also one day stared around the house and wondered what Dominic would say if she told him she'd like to strip the interior out and start from scratch—anything to imprint some little part of herself other than her body on their life, or at least something they could plan together and share in.

It was a couple of days later that she verified something else that might have accounted in part for these impulses, something she hadn't been able to believe in.

Perhaps it was unfortunate that Dominic was with her at the time, which happened to be early one morning when she suddenly got up out of bed and ran to the bathroom to be extremely sick.

'What is it? What's wrong?'

He was up when she came out of the bathroom, weakly wiping her forehead with the back of her hand.

'I ... I'm pregnant.'

CHAPTER EIGHT

IF STEPHANIE had told Dominic she was going to shave her head and paint it blue, she doubted if she could have stunned him more. He froze and his grey eyes widened.

'I don't know how it happened—I'm sorry but...' She opened her hands helplessly.

'Don't know how it happened—I should have thought it was quite obvious,' he said with irony.

Stephanie started to feel cold. 'I mean I don't...know what went wrong; it wasn't *deliberate*,' she said and couldn't control the despair in her voice and had to turn away with her hand to her mouth and dash back to the bathroom.

After a moment he followed her in and wet a towel and wiped her face and hands and neck himself. Then he picked her up and took her back to bed where he simply held her against him until some of the tension left her. Then he said, 'I can't deny this has come as something of a surprise, but have you got anything against being a mother?'

'I...not really. Have you got anything against my being a mother?'

He kissed her forehead and didn't answer directly. 'You don't sound too sure.'

Stephanie hesitated and for a moment longed to be honest and tell him that she had been afraid—not of having a baby, but of being helpless and dependent on him in a way that would make her less able to cope with their incomplete marriage, make her more prone to all sorts of fears and fancies such as the one that was always at the back of her mind anyway—that there was the *right* woman for him somewhere out there, the one who could heal him and claim his total love. And now of course, with his complete shock, more afraid.

'Stephanie?'

She collected her thoughts with an effort but still answered him with some honesty. 'I do want this baby but it's rather strange; I don't feel in command of myself any more—I've got the feeling this is going to bring the real dithery, clumsy side of me back.'

'Then why don't you just let me be in command?' he said wryly. 'Maybe that's how it's supposed to be. For example, right now I command you to relax and stop worrying because I've got plans for today.'

'Today? I thought you were working. It is a week day, isn't it? Or have even the days gone haywire?'

He laughed and kissed her. 'It is a week day,' he assured her. 'But after a suitably restful period in bed I thought we might spend the rest of the day making some plans to do with nurseries, that kind of thing.'

'Oh,' Stephanie said. 'We have months and months——'

'You don't approve?'

'Well, yes, of course!'

'As for a suitably restful period in bed—I still have to demonstrate something to you—settle for once and for all this little matter of the birds and the bees,' he teased and ran his hands down her body. 'There's no evidence of it yet.'

'If you mean I'm still a beanpole,' she said rue-fully, 'I've even lost weight but——'

'But not here,' he said idly, touching her breasts. 'They're still firm and have their same tantalising upcurve beneath and smooth, satiny sweep...'

'Dominic,' she said on a gasping little breath.

His hands stilled. 'Does that hurt?'

'Not...hurt, but they seem to be very sensitive suddenly.'

'I guess if there's one thing I'm going to regret it will be losing my complete mastery of them.' He trailed his hands down to her stomach and then to her hips. 'How about this?'

She looked into his eyes. 'Do you really not mind?' she whispered.

His hand stilled again and his eyes were suddenly sombre. 'How could I mind? I did this to you, remember?'

It wasn't the answer she sought but she knew she'd have to be content with it and, after a long moment of staring down at her searchingly, he began to make love to her. And as always, as his lips sought hers and his hands stroked and ex-plored, her *alter ego* as she sometimes thought of it, responded and flowered and she calmed and concentrated on this act, this matching of their dif-ferences that was for her a never-failing source of delight. This intimacy between them that was the spar she clung to hoping against fervent hope that his ownership of her body and her passion would one day forge the final link between them. And she told herself that that moment of frozen surprise need not necessarily be indicative of anything but that she had taken him by surprise—after all, she'd surprised herself.

In fact, over the next months, instead of getting harder, her life got easier. She still watched her step, she still took nothing about their marriage for granted—she'd learnt that lesson the hard way— but Dominic was undoubtedly more considerate and, whether it was something as simple as planning a nursery or something as nebulous at this stage as providing an heir to the name, her antipathy towards the house faded. Had it been childish in the first place? she wondered.

Then the news came.

'I got a letter from Warwick today. The first four boats have arrived; everyone is intrigued with the design—for which your brother Mike can take a bow...'

'I'm so happy!'

'Yes, he certainly has some good ideas and I don't know if he's mentioned it to you but I think his love life might be getting serious.' Dominic raised an eyebrow at her.

'Yes.' Stephanie grinned. 'He was telling me about her last week. She sounds quite different from his usual type.'

'I got introduced yesterday. She came to see him at lunchtime. A little mouse of a girl on first impression, nervous and very shy, but when she smiles she's rather pretty. Talking of girls...'

'I thought we were talking about boats.'

'The two subjects are related in this case, Mrs Rayburn—incidentally, you're looking rather girlish yourself, certainly still slim and lissom. When is there going to be any evidence for the world to see that my heir is on the way?'

'The way I keep losing my breakfast,' Stephanie said gloomily, 'I don't know. But it's only five months and your mother assures me I must start to pop out soon. In fact I have if you know what to look for. Are you actually looking forward to a much larger me?'

He said quite seriously, 'I think you might be easier to control.'

'Control!'

He laughed at her expression. 'You're already showing signs of it. You don't escape into your own little world nearly so often these days.'

Stephanie looked injured then she had to smile. 'My painting seems to be taking a back seat at the moment. The side-effects of maternity are very curious, you know,' she added.

'I do indeed. I'm thinking of installing an ice-cream machine.'

'I didn't mean that—it's also really hot,' she defended herself and her growing passion for smooth, glorious, plain vanilla ice-cream. Then she grimaced and said ruefully, 'I really thought that was an old wives' tale. But go on about the girls or the boats, I'm not sure *what* you're talking about now!'

'In his letter, Warwick mentioned that his daughter Jennifer has graduated and turned twenty-one in the same breath virtually, and he's giving her a trip to Australia to celebrate. She's definitely coming to Brisbane.'

'Oh, that's great!'

'That's what I thought—in fact, I thought we might ask her to stay with us. Apparently she has plenty of time. What do you think?'

'I think, if she's half as nice as her father, and half the honey he reckons she is, it's a very good idea.'

And the next morning, as if someone had waved a magic wand over her digestive system, she consumed and kept down a large, healthy breakfast, causing her husband to say, 'Perhaps we ought to make preparations for twins?'

A month later Jenny Patterson arrived and Stephanie remembered her father's description of her so clearly. For there were his words duplicated in the flesh—sparkling dark eyes in a delicate beautiful oval face. Long, shining brown hair. A lovely figure; in fact Warwick's beloved daughter was exquisite but so much more; a warm, bubbling personality that was impossible to resist. And, by the time she'd spent three days with them, a rapport had been achieved that had echoed Warwick's words, 'You could even be kindred spirits.' How had he known? Stephanie wondered. How had he known she would be able to talk to me about Veronica and cry out the long-bottled-up tears of remorse because she'd hated her stepmother and come close to hating her father and had said the most awful things to him instead of trying to understand him? Instead of realising how lonely he was and getting on with her own life . . .

'Jenny, Jenny,' Stephanie had said softly, 'you mustn't blame yourself. I'm sure he's told you that and what he was looking for was probably bound up with all sorts of things; reassurance he wasn't getting old—just being human.'

'I suppose so,' Jenny had gulped. 'He said you might understand better than most. He said she tried to victimise you too but you were the one who really made him see what she was.'

And Stephanie had thought, How strange that in my own particular turmoil—perhaps that's what did it—I should have been able to reach someone else who was also suffering...

The two weeks originally planned stretched to three then Jenny went away and saw some more of Australia and came back six weeks later, brown as a berry which suited her and full of vitality and enthusiasm for the land down under.

'The Australian tourist corporation should get hold of you,' Dominic said with a grin, when, after only having been back for half an hour, she'd talked non-stop about what she'd seen.

'Oh, sorry,' she apologised and turned to Stephanie. 'But what is *this*? You've really grown, Stephie, darling!'

Stephanie conceded that she had and Dominic said gravely that they were seriously expecting twins now.

'We are not!' Stephanie contradicted as Jenny's eyes widened. 'Don't take any notice of him. He delights in teasing me these days.'

'You're not the only one he teases,' Jenny confided, putting her arm around Stephanie then tilting her chin at Dominic. 'But it's two against one now, Mr Rayburn. That is...' she lowered her chin and her eyes sparkled ruefully '...I do have a favour to ask first. Could you bear to put up with me for just a little longer? I have this half-finished painting of Ayers Rock—it's to be a present for Daddy and I thought your garden or Stephanie's studio would be the ideal place to finish it off—but I would repay you in every way I can.'

'Oh? How?' Dominic enquired.

'I'd make the beds, do the dishes, hang out the washing...'

'As well as ganging up on me with my wife. I see.' He stared at her thoughtfully. 'I'm not sure what I would get out of this bargain.'

Jenny pretended to be utterly downcast for a moment but she whispered something to Stephanie to which Stephanie replied that he certainly was.

'Certainly am what?' Dominic demanded.

'Having me on,' Jenny said airily. 'I must admit you do do it beautifully, though, and I used to *tremble* to think how unkind you could be if you set your mind to it. I was quite sure you were one of those dark, damning and dangerous men underneath,' she said with a shiver. 'But really, you're very nice.'

Dominic's expression during this speech caused a little chuckle to rise to Stephanie's lips, then, suddenly, he was laughing, they all were, and he ruffled Jenny's hair and remarked that he was glad he was not her father or husband because he suspected she could wring blood out of a stone...

'No, I really don't mind having her,' Stephanie said later that night in bed. 'It's like having a younger sister. She brightens my days, she's reactivated my interest in painting and she's amazingly concerned about getting together a layette and all the right equipment for your heir, not to mention what I should or should not be doing, eating, et cetera, et cetera. She's in fact a mine of information on being pregnant and babies. I asked her where she got it all from and she told me very seriously that she thought one should prepare for these things as well as one could.'

'She's certainly an original,' he commented. 'I'm glad you've got some feminine company; it must help.'

Stephanie moved her swollen body to a more comfortable position and said drowsily, 'Yes. Perhaps we both feel . . . we're repaying Warwick a little, also.'

'That too,' he murmured and began to rub her back.

'That's lovely,' she said softly.

'I'm glad I have some uses in this matriarchal society,' he said gravely.

'Didn't you know—it all still revolves around you? This matriarch-to-be does, anyway. She'd be quite lost without you, I'm afraid . . .'

But once again those proved to be famous last words, although their impact was rather different.

Because of Stephanie's growing lack of mobility they spent the next couple of weeks quietly then, unexpectedly, Melissa took a hand. Having heard about Jenny from her mother who was a frequent visitor to the house in Ascot and who was demonstrating increasing delight about becoming a grandmother, she descended on Stephanie and Jenny one morning, obviously liked what she saw

of the American girl and put herself out to be unusually charming. She did more: somewhat to
Stephanie's annoyance, which she resolutely hid,
she invited Jenny and Dominic to the races the next
day, a Saturday—carefully including Stephanie in
the invitation but saying just a shade doubtfully
that they could surely find somewhere for her to
sit quietly.

Despite herself, Stephanie had to laugh. 'No,
thanks, Melissa. I feel ungainly enough as it is. But
you two go,' she said to Dominic and Jenny.

They'd gone and Jenny had come home bubbling with enthusiasm as well as more invitations.

But she stopped mid-stream and looked at
Stephanie anxiously. And said, 'I feel...as if I'm
deserting you.'

'No, you're not.' Stephanie smiled at her affec-
tionately. 'Go out and enjoy yourself. I'm quite
happy doing what I'm doing.' And indeed she was
as, for some reason, the magic of the Hayman
gardens which she'd sought to capture before, un-
successfully, was flowing on to canvas from her
fingertips and brush. 'It's my time to be quiet but
that doesn't mean you have to. Have some fun!'

Of course, to be absolutely truthful, the prickle
of annoyance which Melissa had aroused re-
mained. But then if she'd ever invited me any-
where, would I have gone? she pondered.

And again, to be absolutely truthful, there were
times when she couldn't help wishing she wasn't so
very pregnant so that it really was uncomfortable
for her to partake in the sightseeing trips Dominic
sometimes took Jenny on, despite her protestations
that it was silly for Jenny not to see as much as she

could while she had the chance. Of course, she reasoned it all out with herself. She knew that Dominic felt a sense of obligation to Warwick because of what had happened with Veronica, and she knew that they both felt that what they were doing for Jenny was a way of redressing that—yet when she stood at the window and watched them come back from these expeditions, generally laughing about something, it was impossible not to feel left out and oddly sad yet annoyed with herself at the same time. And she had to school herself sometimes not to show it. Then she and Dominic had a conversation about Jenny, the significance of which didn't strike her immediately.

'We have a budding socialite in our midst,' Dominic said. 'She's taking Brisbane by storm.'

Stephanie grinned. 'I can believe it.'

He glanced at her, oddly she thought, then hesitated and said, 'Not feeling left out?'

Fortunately she was turned away from him and she had the time to pretend to consider then turn and say with a wry smile, 'You know how I feel about Melissa but no, this is not the time for me to be gadding about. I'm happy to be home, in fact. And I'm happy to see Jenny having such a great time, I really am.'

'We could...' he paused '...have a long line of young men applying to us for her hand, or even have to ring Warwick in a hurry and tell him his daughter has eloped.'

'Not Jenny,' Stephanie said. 'She's a sensible girl—like me.'

'Really?' They were standing together in the kitchen, facing each other but separated by his baby.

'Yes, really!' she said amusedly, but wondered then at something indecipherable in his expression.

'This...' he put his arms about her '...is getting a little difficult.'

Stephanie rested her hands on his arms. 'Not so long now,' she said quietly, looking up into his grey eyes. 'I've been thinking—monogamy must be rather difficult for men at times like this. And then there'll be a few weeks afterwards, too, to cope with.'

'You think some very strange thoughts, sometimes, Mrs Rayburn,' he remarked. 'Are you recommending I go out and get myself a mistress temporarily?' His eyes glinted.

But Stephanie was serious, she realised. 'No,' she said slowly. 'I'm sure I'd hate that but I'm just trying to tell you that I do realise... what it must be like for you.'

'I wonder,' he said enigmatically.

'What do you mean?' she queried.

He slid his hands from her back round to her belly and the baby moved beneath them. He smiled absently and moved them upwards to cup her breasts, now round and full, and said very quietly, his gaze suddenly intent as he stared into her eyes, 'I am sustained and satisfied by the perhaps unworthy assumption that this is all my doing, you see, Stephanie. That's how men survive monogamy at times like this. With typical masculine pride.' He raised his hands to cup her face and stroke back her coppery hair. 'And you're wrong about something else—I still enjoy making love to you. In fact, I'm about to do so right now.'

Which he did and she helped in ways she had not before and reaped the bounty of his pleasure but even that was not enough to wipe out the yearning in her heart for him to have said, with *love* and pride...

And over the next few days she kept thinking of it and she couldn't help remembering that he'd never said anything about love despite the fact that he'd been so considerate and protective during these months.

She was never to understand why she could be so alive to this yet not notice things that might have been apparent to a blind man. Why the first intimation should come as such a shock.

The first intimation came one wet, stormy afternoon when Jenny stared at the streaming kitchen window and sighed. Stephanie was making a casserole for dinner.

'What's up?' she enquired.

'I... I don't really know,' Jenny said with gentle melancholy then smiled ruefully. 'I can't seem to settle to anything. Perhaps, like you, I need to be quiet for a time,' she added thoughtfully. 'Not—I mean these past few weeks have been great but...' She shrugged.

'Perhaps you're getting homesick?' Stephanie suggested.

'No. Stephie—it's hard being a woman, isn't it?'

Stephanie diced some carrots before answering. 'Perhaps,' she said finally. 'I wouldn't have thought the hard times had come for you yet—if they ever do.'

'Do you mean,' Jenny sat opposite in the kitchen chair with her chin in her hands and there was an odd maturity in her eyes, 'that I'm still in the ranks of the girls? Perhaps I am in some respects but I've made some conscious decisions in my life—not to go looking for love being one of them but . . .' She shrugged.

Stephanie frowned and reached for an onion. 'Go on.'

'It's hard to explain—I've got a career in commercial art waiting for me back home but even without looking for it—love—who is to know what I'll be doing in, say, two years from now? Men don't have that uncertainty.'

'If you mean that you might be eight months pregnant and cutting up onions with difficulty . . .' Stephanie rubbed her eyes with her wrists ' . . . yes, I see what you mean.'

'And while it wouldn't be true to say I long to be doing just that—here . . .' she handed Stephanie a clean tea-towel with a grin ' . . . it's always there, isn't it? The lure, no, the thought . . . that when the right man—it would be so terrible if he was the wrong man—comes along, that's what one will be doing, happily, hopefully. Like you. Just pure biology is still against you whatever they say, isn't it?'

'The hankering for a home, a husband, kids? Are you, Jenny?'

Those clear brown eyes, rested on her soberly. 'I think I must be.'

*　　*　　*

No, Stephanie thought, as she served the casserole that evening. No. Why am I thinking this? It's only because she's surrounded by domestic bliss at the moment and it's affecting her generally...not specifically.

But it was still the surprisingly mature, more serious Jenny at dinner with them although the old sparkle did show through once or twice. In response to Dominic...

Stephanie found herself watching them with her heart beating oddly after dinner. They'd insisted she sit down with her feet up and Jenny had cleared the table and done the dishes and brought them coffee.

'Not out on the town tonight, Jenny?' Dominic said, lying back in his chair.

Jenny sank down on to the settee and lifted the hair off the nape of her neck, letting it fall in a shining cloud. 'No,' she replied gravely, and cradled her cup in both hands. 'I'm not really a socialite at heart; a little bit is lovely but I'd rather be here with you two actually.' She shrugged her slim shoulders and stared down at her coffee.

In the silence that followed, for some reason the oval perfection of her face, the twisted grace of her body, the knowledge that she was not a social butterfly but a warm, generous, loving girl with the gift for brightening other people's lives—all of it caused Stephanie's heart to beat oddly again, and caused her to glance at Dominic with the sudden thought in her mind that *this* girl might have been the one. This different girl who made him laugh, who was untouched but not unseasoned, who had handled her life with maturity and intelligence—

and who, dear God, Stephanie thought, is falling in love with him. Does she know it properly yet? Does he...?

The answer was there for her to see in the way Dominic's grey gaze was resting sombrely on Jenny's unconscious face. He knew.

It was perhaps unfortunate that her state of mind made her restless in bed that night so that, as they sometimes did now it was midsummer and hot and breathless and humid, he finally went to sleep in a spare bed. They'd laughed about it the first time but, as she'd pointed out, it was unnecessary for them both to be uncomfortable especially when he had to work and she could rest during the day.

This night, however, she would have given anything for them to be together whatever the conditions, to feel the bulk of him beside her—something tangible to pin her thoughts on instead of the whirling chaos that came once he'd gone.

It stayed with her over the days that followed despite her efforts to quell it.

Of course it took its inevitable toll. She grew clumsy and jumpy again even when she desperately reminded herself that because Jenny had fallen in love it didn't automatically mean Dominic had; but it was much easier to remember the times they'd spent alone, Dominic and Jenny, times out and about doing the kind of things *she* and Dominic had never done, the way his work had taken second place for once, the fact—and this was the bottom line—that she still didn't know if he was making the best of this baby because he had no choice. How could she forget that stunned surprise or his later words...'How could I mind?' which was surely akin to saying, I have no option...

To make matters worse, if Jenny had not completely guessed what was happening to her, it was obviously suddenly hitting her. She grew quieter and tenser in a matter of days—then out of the blue told them she was going home.

'Today—this afternoon,' she said, twisting her hands painfully. 'I...I was just walking past the airline office and...and something came over me and I went in and there's a seat...'

It was Dominic who said quietly, 'You don't have to explain—homesickness is no respecter of times and places—although you'll miss the main event.' He smiled slightly. 'But I've already had two anxious letters from your father. He seems to be worried that you're thinking of making Australia home.'

Jenny clutched at this straw. 'That's why I'm going—oh, Stephie...' she turned anxiously '...you must think I'm crazy not staying for the baby but Dad...well, I've been away long enough; he must be lonely. You *do* understand, don't you?' And her eyes were anguished and pleading.

Stephanie drew a breath and said sincerely and gently, 'Of course, Jenny! But we'll miss you and I'll always owe you a debt of gratitude for making this pregnancy go much more quickly than it would have without you.'

Jenny studied her compulsively for a moment but there were no shadows in Stephanie's eyes, only warmth and affection.

The other girl mumbled something incomprehensible then flung her arms around Stephanie—

or tried to which made them laugh together, then she went off to pack, leaving Stephanie and Dominic alone.

'Well,' Stephanie said lightly. 'I will miss her.' But she sat down rather suddenly.

Dominic frowned. 'Are you all right? You've been——'

'I know,' she said with a grimace. 'Back to my old form but I think this time it's because I'm genuinely heavy and slow and clumsy.' She smiled up at him. 'But it's only two weeks—poor thing...' She gestured towards Jenny's room. 'She feels, or felt, guilty about Warwick and blamed herself for letting him get into Veronica's clutches. I guess she's just had another attack of conscience.'

Dominic looked at her narrowly and was about to speak but Stephanie said serenely, 'Do you think she'll mind if I don't come to the airport? I just don't feel up to it.'

'Stephanie——'

'No,' she broke in firmly, 'I'm perfectly fine but today I just feel as if I'm having triplets at least.'

'Are...' he paused and his grey eyes were probing so that Stephanie held her breath and, by a maximum effort of will, returned his look still serenely '...you quite sure?'

'Quite.'

It was, however, only several hours later, when Dominic had barely returned from seeing Jenny off, when Stephanie stopped what she was doing to look up as he walked in, and stayed stopped, arrested by two things. A curious sense of relief that she would have to act nothing out any longer, and a sense of apprehension.

'She made it,' he said, pulling off his jacket and walking towards her. 'Stephanie——'

But she interrupted him. 'Dominic—I know it's two weeks early and that I'm not the expert biologist in this house but I think . . . your heir is on the way . . .'

Which was true but it was twelve painful hours before he arrived and by then Stephanie's endurance had been stretched to the limit and she could only clasp the bundle they gave her weakly and had no strength left to control her tears of relief, of disbelief that it was over, that the baby was perfect.

She woke later to find Dominic sitting beside the bed and remembered dimly that he had been through it all, remembered suddenly the look of pain in his eyes when the doctor had murmured something about the narrowness of her hips . . . It was still there, she saw as she watched him, staring straight ahead, unaware her eyes had fluttered open, his face pale and weary and curiously lined.

She put out a tentative hand and whispered, 'That's why they make us tough. Don't look like that—I'm all right.'

He turned his head slowly and put his hand over hers and stared down into her eyes. 'If I could,' he said with difficulty, 'have borne that pain for you, I would have gladly.'

She smiled tremulously. 'Thank you for that and for being there.'

He closed his eyes and lifted her hand to his lips and kissed it gently.

'Well—so we're awake!' A nurse bustled in with a bundle. 'Thought it was about time, so I brought young Master Rayburn along to say good day and I'll tell you something else; he has a powerful pair of lungs, don't you, boyo? He's been testing them out,' she said to Stephanie with a beam. 'Here, sit up a bit and take your first real good look at him. Don't be afraid to unwrap him and count all his fingers and toes and give me a buzz if he gets too obstreperous but I'll only be down the corridor making you both a cup of tea. Dad sure looks as if he could do with it!'

Dominic watched her retreating back wryly and said with something of his old amusement, 'I feel as if I've really let the side down. Well.' They both stared down at the baby in Stephanie's arms then at each other with almost identically helpless expressions, and began to laugh.

'I'm not game to disturb so much as a hair of his head,' Stephanie said, still chuckling, 'let alone move a muscle in case he starts exercising his lungs—oh, look!'

One pink fist emerged from the wrapping, although Master Rayburn kept his eyes tightly shut and maintained his expression of severity and disapproval. But the fist opened and waved a little and Stephanie slid her forefinger into it, whereupon five extremely small fingers curled about hers and a slight sound was made—of contentment apparently, as no further movement ensued.

If her new son had clutched her heart-strings, the impact could not have been greater, Stephanie thought dazedly, suddenly absorbing every detail of him she could see and feeling her breasts swell. So entranced was she for the moment that she didn't notice Dominic watching her with another look in his eyes—as if he could clearly see the bond that was being forged beneath his gaze, and could only marvel at it.

Then she looked up and her lips quivered as she said softly, 'So this is how they get you in again and again!'

'Does it . . .' he paused and searched her face, the new light in her eyes ' . . . make it worthwhile?'

She didn't have to answer.

All of which took her mind off Jenny and the pretence of ignorance she'd assumed—to an extent. But when she did think of it, it was to think that for all concerned she'd done the right thing.

Nor, over the next days, did Dominic mention it.

In fact it was Melissa who did . . .

'Well,' she said, depositing a parcel and a bunch of roses on Stephanie's bed, 'I hear you've decided to call my nephew Nicholas.'

Whether this was an overture of some kind or not, Stephanie decided to treat it as such. 'Yes. After my father but, as you'll no doubt see for yourself, the most striking resemblance your nephew bears . . .' she smiled rather ruefully ' . . . is to your brother.'

Melissa peered into the bassinet beside the bed. 'So I see,' she said after a time. 'I wonder if he'll be as autocratic?'

'They're already calling him Nicholas the First, around here.'

Melissa laughed, to do her credit, and proceeded to make all the right enquiries, even to glance repeatedly at the bassinet with unwitting fascination in her eyes until she said prosaically that there was obviously something about new babies that got you in.

'I have to agree,' Stephanie murmured.

'But Jenny...didn't stay to see this one,' Melissa added, her grey eyes resting on Stephanie thoughtfully.

'No, she left a couple of days ago——'

'I know—I saw them at the airport. Rather sudden, wasn't it?'

'I suppose so,' Stephanie said reluctantly and stared at her sister-in-law with her nerves prickling suddenly.

There was a long silence then Melissa said rather unsteadily, 'They were embracing. They—I'd gone to see someone else off and they...didn't know I was there.'

It amazed Stephanie how steady *her* voice was. 'Were they? Dominic is very fond of Jenny and we both know her father.'

To her utter surprise, Melissa's eyes suddenly filled with angry tears and she got up abruptly and strode over to the window, dashing at them angrily. Then she turned and said bitterly, 'There's something about you, Stephanie, that brings out the worst in me. And, if you must know, right at this moment, I'm...as jealous as hell!'

Stephanie's lips parted soundlessly. But for once, it seemed, Melissa was prepared to be honest.

'You know why I'm jealous, don't you?' she demanded.

And when Stephanie could only look at her bewilderedly, she went on in the same queer, angry voice, 'Because *I'm* the one out in the cold now! The three of you, now *four* of you . . . oh, hell.' She turned away bleakly.

'You mean...' Stephanie licked her lips '...your mother and Dominic and... Melissa, it doesn't have to be that way.'

It was a long time before Melissa turned again then she did so with a sigh. 'But I've been such a bitch! And now I've even set out to make mischief.'

'Do you mean they weren't——?'

'No, they were, but,' she shrugged, 'it was probably only as you said. Stephanie,' she paused, and there was something curiously pleading in her eyes, '*could* we . . . be friends?'

It was Nicholas the First who helped his mother out. He gave a peremptory wail which stopped his aunt in her tracks and then once again, as if drawn by a magnet, she approached the bassinet.

'Pick him up,' Stephanie said gently.

'A small miracle happened this afternoon,' she said to Dominic that evening, and told him about Melissa.

He raised his eyebrows and grinned then said, 'You're very forgiving, Stephanie.'

Stephanie considered. 'Well, I know what it's like to feel an . . . outsider.'

He picked up her hand. 'I trust you no longer feel that way,' he said soberly.

'I . . . no.' She smiled faintly. 'So, everything in the garden is lovely at the moment.' But she watched his hand about hers, not his eyes, which would have been useless anyway, because she'd never been able to read the true state of his heart from his eyes.

He said, with amusement, 'You obviously have green fingers.'

CHAPTER NINE

'I KNOW three months is not any great time to be forming unshakeable convictions,' Stephanie said one cool evening, 'but your son and heir is going to be athletic.'

Dominic grinned. 'Like his father,' he said complacently.

'According to his grandmother, not even his matchless father was as active at this age,' she retorted.

'His grandmother is besotted—as his mother is although she tries to hide it. But he could well be artistic—it's definitely too early to be forming convictions about that.'

'Oh, I don't know,' Stephanie murmured. 'The way he captures the heart of everyone who lays eyes on him is just pure artistry sometimes, especially now he's got the art of smiling...down to a fine art. It's almost cool enough for a fire in the evenings now.' She yawned and raised her hands above her head in a weary stretch.

'Come here,' Dominic said quietly and after the barest hesitation she went and curled up beside him on the settee. 'You've gone thin again, except for your breasts,' he said after a time.

'I think I was born to be thin,' she murmured.

'You don't think my son and heir is wearing you down a little?'

She looked up. 'I . . . what do you mean?'

'Well, you've given him a great start—perhaps it's time to put him on a bottle.'

'But I feel fine! I know I get tired easily but——'

'You also find it hard to relax.'

Stephanie was silent, because it was true, and her heart started to beat heavily in case he should ever divine *why* it was true—of which the demands of his son were only a part. 'I enjoy feeding him,' she said slowly. 'Do you . . .? I mean . . .' She hesitated, wondering how she could keep the subject safe then finding herself wondering suddenly what was really in his mind. 'Do you think it's interfering with our love life?' she heard herself ask before she could stop herself.

He took her hand. 'There's a time and tide for all things,' he said and smiled slightly. 'Not very original but probably true. The tide of our love life has to ebb and flow like all tides. But I think I know you well enough to know—that it's not flowing at all for you at the moment.'

She lowered her lashes on the sudden stricken look of confusion in her eyes. And it ran through her mind that the sooner she stopped trying to deceive him, about anything, the better, because if nothing else she was wasting her time. But how to tell him she was haunted? Haunted by Jenny. Plagued, even in his arms, by visions of the American girl, her charm, her wit, her smooth lovely figure, the two of them embracing at the airport . . .

'Stephanie,' he said quietly, 'look at me.'

She did, reluctantly.

'It could be quite normal. Your body has made enormous physical adjustments, your whole life has changed and postnatal trauma is by no means unknown—even to a layman like myself. If that's what it is then I only want to do all in my power to help. If there's anything else, though, I need to know.' His grey eyes were sober and probing. 'For example, if you feel our marriage isn't working?'

Speak now or forever hold your peace... The phrase slid through Stephanie's mind from nowhere, but how appropriate, she thought as a succession of pros and cons flashed after it. Speak and perhaps reveal yourself as untrusting, say it all and feel as if you're defiling us all somehow, including Jenny, tell him that it's *working*, this marriage, but it still lacks the inescapable, unreasonable, unchangeable love that Jenny might be able to bring to him. But, while you may be able to hold your peace verbally, aren't your nerves already betraying you? And why Jenny? Because he didn't tell you he knew she'd fallen in love with him? But you went out of your way to avoid having him tell you...

'It's important for another reason,' he said then. 'I have to go overseas for a few weeks. Singapore and the States. Unfortunately, it will be an impossibly tight schedule—too tight for you and Nicky to enjoy it.'

He was still holding her hand and her fingers moved then relaxed. 'I'll be fine,' she said huskily but her eyes were quite steady. 'And I'll take your advice. From now on instead of striving to be the perfect mother, I'll...' her lips quivered into a smile '...relax. I might even start painting again.'

But despite her resolution to hold her peace, and other resolutions, the night before he left did not go according to plan. She was tense when she'd so desperately wanted to be loving and calm, in bed with him, then the baby woke and kept on waking on and off through the night.

'There doesn't seem to be anything wrong with him,' she said anxiously, finally bringing him back to their bed with her. 'He hasn't got a temperature, his tummy's not upset and he's too young to be teething.'

Dominic moved over and lay on his side propped on an elbow. 'Perhaps he guessed what his parents had in mind for this night, and took exception to being relegated from the forefront of our minds.'

But although Stephanie smiled, it was worriedly. 'Do you think I spoil him?'

'Yes,' Dominic said with a grin, 'although it's debatable whether one can spoil a three-month-old baby. But look, he's calmed down. Why don't you bring his pram in and put it beside the bed? That way we might all get some sleep.'

She did and placed it where she could reach it and Nicholas Rayburn obligingly went to sleep, leaving his mother wide awake, however, and miserable.

'This... *isn't* what I planned,' she said unhappily some time later, lying in Dominic's arms but chastely.

'What do they say about the best-laid plans of mice and men? Perhaps our reunion night will be more successful.'

'Don't you mind?' she said jerkily.

He moved and smoothed her hair. 'Do you really envisage me as someone who can't do without it on a very regular basis?'

'They say...for men...that it's difficult.' She winced as she felt him laughing silently.

He replied, 'It may be difficult; it's not impossible. I'll survive but you...' His voice changed. 'You made me a promise, you know. To relax. In other words, go to sleep, Mrs Rayburn; you're working yourself into a state about nothing.'

Stephanie subsided, but, if anything, felt worse. Especially when Dominic fell asleep not long afterwards and she was tormented by a new thought—how could he be content with their love life the way it was after the way it had been, especially after making it so clear to her that it was the only role for her that mattered to him? Surely his patience with what he thought was a touch of postnatal trauma must be wearing a bit thin. Or was his undoubted restraint the result of something else altogether—such as the desire to have someone else in his arms?

Then his departure was only a few hours away and in the inevitable last-minute rush to get Nicholas ready for the trip to the airport, et cetera, there was no time for anything but the basics—yet time to notice that she looked a wreck, thin and with dark shadows under her eyes which she tried to conceal.

But somehow she managed to put on a brave front and was aided by the arrival of his mother at the airport to see him off too, and to reassure him his wife and son would have plenty of back-up if needed in his absence.

Stephanie detected a rather wry light in his grey eyes as he surveyed them all and also a slightly faraway look which hurt her to the core, but in the short time left to her before his flight was called although she desperately wanted to she could find no words, no way of communicating with him properly.

So her drive home from the airport, having assured his mother that she would be quite all right and there was no need to cancel her weekly golf afternoon on their account, was characterised by a supreme feeling of failure. And the bitter thought that *their* last embrace had been awkward and un-revealing of her love because she'd been trying so hard to continue the pretence that she *wasn't* wondering not only whether he was going to see Jenny but how he could feel anything for her, anyway.

If anything good came out of the rest of the day, it was that she wasn't allowed to dwell on her bitter thoughts. For it became plain that Nicky had acquired a temperature. And although a visit to the doctor brought to light only a very mild, childish ailment, her son was fractious for the rest of the day and night, although he woke the following morning obviously restored to blooming health and good temper.

That was when the full extent of all her doubts and miseries came back to plague her, and on top of it she'd had no call from Dominic to say he'd arrived, if nothing else. Of course he's arrived, she thought wretchedly, but wouldn't it be natural to ring me?

She always knew that it was a spurious gesture of defiance that made her come to a sudden decision—she would go and spend a few days with Nan. Why not? Let him wonder and worry where she was if he did try to ring. She had no idea what it was going to cost her.

Accordingly, she was sitting at the kitchen table drinking a cup of tea and waiting for Nicky to wake, with several packed bags beside her, when she heard a car pull up and then familiar footsteps down the hallway.

It was Dominic, his face weary and lined, his eyes inscrutable.

'Why...what...?' She scrambled up and knocked her cup over.

He ignored the trickles of tea spilling on to the floor. Instead his gaze lingered on the bags and when his eyes came back to her face they were shockingly mocking and inimical. 'I might have known,' he said softly but with a curious insolence. 'I did know—that's why I'm here.'

'Kn-know what?' she stammered.

'That you were about to do one of your disappearing acts, dear Stephanie.' He shrugged and leant his shoulders against the door-frame. 'I'm sure you feel you have good reason—you always did. Why don't you give me one of your enlightening lectures? I have the feeling that, this time, it has something to do with trust. Or the lack of it,' he said with irony. 'Because you can't help being quite convinced I was on my way to...' he paused '...throw myself into Jenny Patterson's arms.'

Shock darkened her own eyes. 'You knew—I knew!' The whispered words were out before she could stop them or consider their implication.

'I know you a lot better than you think,' he said roughly. 'I know you well enough to know that it's the kind of thing you'd allow to fester in your mind and brood over.'

She gasped and her mind reeled with guilt and pain yet also the seeds of anger but he went on mercilessly, 'And that then you'd let your famous pride take charge and that you'd most likely convince yourself you were better off without me—who needs a two-timing husband, after all?—but least of all *you* who always thought you could do without one anyway, after I'd... initiated you into the mysteries of sex, that is. Oh, excepting that it was handy to have me around to top up your creative processes, wasn't it?'

'Dominic...' Her eyes were horrified and shock prevented her from getting together the words to refute him.

'Am I wrong?' he drawled, looking at the bags on the floor again.

'*Yes...*'

'You didn't wonder about me and Jenny?' he shot at her.

Her lips parted. 'I... yes, I did, but——'

'And you weren't all set to do a little disappearing act?'

'I...' A flood of colour poured into her cheeks.

'That tells its own tale, o, ye of little faith,' he said with that scalding, soft insolence again. 'It's a pity you blush so easily, Stephanie,' he added. 'You give yourself away every time. Now listen,' he straightened and came across to her at last, so that he seemed to be towering over her and she took an uncertain step backwards '...whatever else you like to think about me, you and I have a commitment—we have a verbal commitment that's now translated itself into a human one and I presume he's asleep—and we'll honour that commitment. If...' he paused and watched the growing storm in her eyes, and went on in the same hard, clipped tones '...behind closed doors you would like our marriage to be what it once was, what you convinced yourself it was—a sort of forced march with me doing all the forcing—if that's how you really *like* it, I shall oblige as I always did. But to all other intents and purposes and for Nicky's sake we will go on in unity.'

The red mist that swam before Stephanie's eyes didn't, curiously, impede her aim. She hit him hard and accurately on the cheekbone and stung her hand probably as much as she did him.

But after a moment, during which his eyes went dark and frighteningly savage, he laughed softly. 'A good way to begin,' he murmured and swung her up into his arms.

'Dominic...'

He ignored her spoken protest and her frenzied attempts to free herself and carried her to their bedroom where he threw her down on the bed and closed the door deliberately.

'You bastard, you can't do this!' she panted, trying to get to her knees but hampered by her skirt.

'Yes, I can.' He glanced at her wryly and shrugged his jacket off then his tie and started to unbutton his shirt. 'I always could——'

She reached for the clock on the bedside table, the only thing handy, and flung it at him. It missed and landed on the carpet with a dull clunk. He picked it up unhurriedly, glanced at it and shook it with a grimace. 'We might have to denude this room of missiles. It could become quite expensive,' he said with a faint smile.

'You...*you're* enjoying this,' she cried incredulously.

'Am I?' He pulled off his shirt and approached the bed. 'I wonder if it has anything to do...' he paused meditatively '...with how much you'll be enjoying yourself shortly, Stephanie. Relax,' he said barely audibly and sat down on the bed. 'Why fight it? That part was always only the preliminary.'

'Oh, God,' she whispered, tears of despair and disbelief suddenly brimming over.

'That's better,' he murmured and took her shoulders in his hands and drew her into his arms. 'Did you honestly think I'd let you take away my son, Stephanie?' he went on, sliding his fingers down her blouse and freeing the buttons one by one. 'I thought you knew that we Rayburns have our own kind of pride.' He slipped the cotton blouse off her shoulders and stared down at her breasts and bra. Then he lifted his eyes to hers and they were supremely mocking. He went on, with a suddenly lifted eyebrow as he eased her upright, removed the blouse fully and reached behind her, 'Considering the number of times I've done this to you I would have thought that by now you'd have invested in some front-opening bras. But there...' he unhooked it and slid the straps down her arms, freeing her breasts and trailing his fingers across her nipples '...not such a hassle.' He raised his eyes to hers again.

'Dominic...' She stared into those grey depths. 'Don't...do this to me.'

'Unfortunately...' his voice was suddenly hard again '...it's too late for me to stop now. Perhaps you can comfort yourself with the knowledge that you have no choice left—unless you're really feeling deeply wronged.' He slid his hands up her back into her hair and drew her head back. Then his mouth descended on hers.

When he finally stopped kissing her, her lips were bruised and swollen and her breathing ragged but something told her that to fight him further would only be dangerous, that there was a depth to his mood that made her shiver to contemplate and where, before, in her anger, she'd thought she'd rather die than explain anything to him, now she wondered dimly if she could communicate anything to him at all.

He laid her back against the pillows and finished undressing her in silence then took the rest of his clothes off with economic precision and she lay motionless, praying for some deliverance from this deliberate act of possession. Praying for Nicky to wake up, but it was obvious the trauma of being so fractious the day before had tired him right out.

It was also soon obvious that even if it was only an act of possession she was not going to be allowed even the small luxury of passive resistance although her hurt was so great at the things he'd said that she certainly couldn't be accused of responding readily. In fact for a long time her body seemed numbed to the things he did to her—not precisely brutally yet calculatedly—but when he took her at last with a driving need she couldn't deny the climax he inflicted on her and they were united in a physical release that stunned her almost as much as their mental disunity and total disarray had.

And he knew, as he always had, that he'd wrung the final response from her—it was there, not in what he said but in his eyes as he stared down at her.

She turned her head away and tears of humiliation slid on to the pillow.

She didn't turn when she felt him get up; she lay with her eyes closed for some minutes, then, because it was so quiet, thought he must have left the room without her hearing. But he was still there, standing at the window with his back to her, staring out over the garden, a sombre, still menacing presence—and there might have been a million miles between them.

The doorbell rang.

He swore softly, glanced at her over his shoulder then pulled a pair of shorts out of his bureau and went to answer it, all but closing the bedroom door.

It didn't stop her from hearing the conversation that ensued; she'd never had any trouble hearing his sister Melissa...

'Dominic! You're not supposed to be here!'

'Nevertheless I am,' he drawled. 'What brings *you* here and have you come to stay? Or are you merely carrying your bags around for fun?'

Stephanie's lips parted and she sat up.

'Don't be sarcastic, Dom. If you recall I had a cold so I haven't been able to see my nephew for a while but now I'm over it and seeing Stephanie's alone—or was supposed to be—I thought I'd come and spend a few days with her.' Melissa's tone had grown quite belligerent as she spoke.

'You really surprise me sometimes, Melissa,' her brother remarked, 'but why not?'

'Why *are* you here, though?' Melissa demanded.

'Something came up and I had to cancel the trip and return, posthaste,' he said with a cynical undertone that was not lost on Stephanie. She closed her eyes and wondered a little wildly what else could go wrong for her today and why Melissa, despite her about-face, could still be enough of her old self to simply arrive and never think of asking first—although, she reminded herself, that was what she'd been about to do to Nan. But surely he wouldn't...?

He did. 'You're very welcome though, dear sister mine. I'm sure Stephanie could use some...help.'

'Where is Stephanie?' Melissa sounded mollified but ever so slightly suspicious.

'Stephanie is...lying down,' Dominic said. 'It's an old trick of motherhood. When the baby sleeps you're wise to catch a nap yourself to compensate for all the times you don't sleep. Bear it in mind——'

He stopped as a sound issued from the nursery—Nicky was awake. That sealed things for Melissa.

'Oh, don't wake Stephanie,' she said eagerly. 'I can cope. I'm really quite good with him now.'

'He could be hungry,' Dominic pointed out.

'Then I'll placate him for a while,' Melissa said airily and with all her old assurance. 'You can put my bags in my old room, Dom.' Footsteps proceeded down the passage.

'At your service,' Dominic murmured.

Stephanie lay back with her hands to her face then she got up.

She was in their en-suite shower when he came back to the bedroom and he simply entered and pulled the glass door open.

Stephanie gasped, reached out a little blindly to turn the water off then just stood there as his hard gaze travelled over her satiny, dripping body.

'You heard?' he said at last.

She nodded.

'Fortunately she's so busy gooing and cooing, that I got *your* bags back here without her noticing—are you all right?' he said abruptly.

She licked drops of water off her lips. 'No,' she whispered. 'No, I'm not, and if you think I can put any sort of a face on it for *days* for your sister of all people——'

'You should have thought of that before you won her over so completely,' he said ironically. 'You really should stop and think of the consequences of your actions more often, Stephanie, then we might not be in this mess. But what I said earlier stands, so you'd better practise some kind of a brave face, my dear, because you have about ten minutes before Nicky starts bawling with hunger. I meant,' he said with a curious, barely controlled savagery, 'did I hurt you physically? I *know* you can't be all right otherwise.'

For an instant Stephanie couldn't help wondering if he wished he had. 'Would you care...?'

'Yes, I'd care——'

'Why?'

'Because I'm no longer prepared to allow you to hold secret...' his eyes mocked her '...grudges against me. Tell me,' he ordered.

'Then for your comfort,' she said quietly and deliberately and in what she hoped was an equally mocking parody of what he'd once said to her, 'no. But I have to warn you, Dominic; you'll never be able to do that to me again *without* hurting me.'

He smiled drily. 'We'll see. Finished?' He handed her a towel. 'Would you mind if I had a shower now?'

She put the towel to her face. 'Dominic...'

But he only waited impassively and it suddenly dawned on her that he must have been travelling for hours and hours or waiting around at airports...

She stepped out, hesitated, her eyes searching his, but they were harder than she'd ever seen them, and she turned away convulsively.

CHAPTER TEN

THE next endless days were the hardest of Stephanie's life.

How she did put a brave face on things she never knew, but she suspected that her much maligned pride helped. She also wondered if she'd ever forget the things Dominic had said to her, how he'd twisted all the things she'd told him, how he'd revealed that he'd never really revised his first opinions of her motivations.

Added to this was her own guilt, despite the fact that she *hadn't* been planning to leave him. Guilt because of her lack of faith, she couldn't deny that, although her grounds for it lay in him himself and it wasn't so much that she'd believed he'd be deliberately unfaithful to her. Now, too, she had to wonder whether this savage reaction hadn't been prompted by his own sense of guilt.

On top of her despised pride, Melissa undoubtedly helped at first. Not given to much introspection herself, she took others very much for granted and had become so absorbed in babies or at least one baby that she had little time to stop and realise there was an atmosphere you could cut with a knife about her—or so Stephanie felt.

Not that Dominic spent much time at home and the only times he and Stephanie spent alone were at night, in bed. Nights of tension when she lay beside him, stiff and fearful in case he'd make good his threat—more fearful, perhaps, that he would be able to do it without hurting her, as he always had been able to. Nights of telling herself there was a lot she could and should try to explain but of being unable to feel anything but helpless and hopeless in the face of the stone wall of his indifference now—he barely spoke to her, let alone tried to touch her.

Then the awful, insidious tension started to crack her defences obliquely. Her milk began to be affected.

'You're not a very happy boy today, Nicky!' Melissa said exasperatedly. 'Do you think he's teething, Stephanie?'

'He's not even four months old—I think he's hungry but I only fed him two hours ago.'

'Well, feed him again!' Melissa said with a touch of her old imperiousness. And there followed a day and a half of trauma before Stephanie was forced to admit that she would have to supplement his feeds.

It was late that night when Dominic came home, and found her in the kitchen making up bottles. Melissa had gone to bed and Nicky, thankfully, was asleep too.

He flung his briefcase on the kitchen table and flexed his shoulders wearily. Stephanie, after a glance at him that told her nothing had changed, turned back to her task.

He opened the fridge, took out a can of beer, pulled off his tie and sat down at the kitchen table. It was only then that his eyes narrowed on her.

'What are you doing?' he said abruptly.

'What it looks like,' she replied quietly, not turning.

'Stephanie—look at me!' he commanded.

She brushed her hair off her forehead with her wrist and turned at last.

She had on a long-sleeved black blouse tucked into cream jeans and the black accentuated her pallor but brought out the copper in her hair. Her feet were bare and there were shadows like thumb-prints beneath her eyes. The jeans moulded her slenderness and there was an air of tired fragility about her.

He took it all in, including the unspoken acceptance in her eyes that he was not about to be kind.

'Why have you put him on the bottle?' he said curtly. 'I thought you enjoyed feeding him.'

She shrugged. 'He seems to need it.'

'Why?'

'Do I have to spell it out?' she murmured. 'There just isn't enough milk any more.'

'For which you blame me, no doubt,' he said roughly.

'No.' She thought for a bit then turned back to the bottles. 'I think I blame me—my brave face just isn't brave enough——' She stopped with a jerk because he'd got up swiftly and was standing right behind her.

But she stayed, facing the counter for a moment, then she pushed her hair behind her ears and turned warily. Their gazes clashed and held and into hers crept an unwitting plea, but nothing changed and he had never more so reminded her of a dark, sardonic captor than in those tortured moments before he turned away, picked up his beer and drained it, and walked out of the room.

It was more than she could do to spend the night with him, she knew, so she made up the small bed in Nicky's room and thought she had a good enough excuse should Melissa make any enquiries, although she doubted she would. Then she thought that she would have to do something about Melissa if she still showed no signs of wanting to leave tomorrow; she just couldn't go on like this.

Dominic did not query her absence at all.

In fact Melissa proved belatedly intuitive the next morning, a Sunday.

It was while Dominic was outside doing something to the pool filter that she said abruptly to Stephanie, 'Am I imagining things or are you two having some sort of crisis?'

Stephanie coloured and grimaced.

'Is it serious?' Melissa demanded.

'Melissa——' Stephanie said with an effort but was not allowed to go on.

'Stephanie,' Melissa said grimly, 'please tell me it has nothing to do with what *I* told you about Dom and Jenny at the airport—that day after Nicky was born. I still feel guilty enough about trying to put the wrong interpretation on it.'

'It ...' Stephanie said with difficulty. 'Melissa, all marriages go through this from time to time I'm sure but——'

'You're not thinking of leaving him?'

'No... No, of course not,' Stephanie said and hoped the irony of things hadn't shown in her voice.

'Would you like me to go, then?'

Stephanie smiled sketchily. 'I would hate you to think I'm chasing you away, I do so appreciate how you are with Nicky, but ...'

'Of course I understand all that,' Melissa said impatiently. 'I *can't* understand why neither of you simply said to me, we're in the middle of a God Almighty scrap—I'm not an idiot, you know!'

'We do know, Melissa,' a voice said behind them, causing them both to turn abruptly. Dominic stood in the doorway and he smiled rather drily at his sister. 'Sorry, it was my fault.'

'Well,' Melissa said, 'I'll be on my bicycle.' She seemed about to say something else and she glanced piercingly at Stephanie for a long moment but, for once in her life, obviously decided not to speak her mind although she did say, with an attempt at light-heartedness and a faint grin, 'Let me know when it's all right to come back!'

'What did she tell you about me and Jenny at the airport?'

Melissa had barely left when the question came.

Stephanie drew a startled breath. 'How...?'

'I happened to be at the tap below the window during your conversation.'

'Oh. She...said she was surprised that Jenny should be leaving so unexpectedly.'

'Go on. I'm sure there was more.' He was watching her like a hawk, she realised.

'Look, Melissa and I——'

'Have sorted out your differences, I know,' he said coolly. 'Was that before or after she—wilfully misinterpreted what she saw at the airport?'

'Dominic—afterwards,' Stephanie admitted.

'All the same, it added fuel to your suspicions—when did you decide Jenny was in love with me, Stephanie?'

Nothing could be much worse than this hard, cold interrogation, she decided, but at least it was a communication of its kind, so she gathered the Sunday papers she'd been reading in the lounge, folded them, leant back in her chair and tucked her feet beneath her. It was a bright, chilly morning and Dominic had on a grey tracksuit and, after his bout with the pool filter and fresh air, he looked alert and as if all his senses were honed—honed to demolish her yet again, she thought with a shiver and thought desolately that all she could do was be honest.

'Perhaps I was a bit blind,' she said slowly, 'but not until a few days before she left.'

He strolled over to the fireplace and leant absently against the mantelpiece. 'Why didn't you tell me? Why did you so resolutely pretend you didn't know? Especially after Melissa gave you real cause for doubt, I gather,' he said with irony.

'Why didn't *you* . . .?' She broke off and tried to compose herself to match his containment. 'How long did you know?' she asked.

He moved his shoulders. 'If you hadn't been enjoying her company so much I would have sent her home sooner,' he said thoughtfully. 'But I didn't really expect it to get to the stage it did. Not once she started going out and about. Nor, since you're wondering, is it the easiest thing in the world to explain to your pregnant wife that her best friend is falling in love with you. And sometimes I even wondered if I was imagining it, especially when you were so content. I also told myself it was highly unlikely both Warwick's wife and his daughter . . .' His lips twisted. 'Well, let's say it's the kind of situation you do find unlikely and pray to God isn't happening,' he said drily.

Stephanie half smiled.

'What's that supposed to mean?' he queried acidly.

She thought for a moment. 'That Warwick's daughter is nothing like his second wife was and that—you've had women falling in love with you half your life so there was nothing very unlikely about it to my mind.'

'So,' he drawled, 'let's proceed to the next step. The scales fell from your eyes, Melissa did her bit, but for a while you really fooled me. I thought your saying nothing was your way of saying, it happened, it's over and best left unsaid—I trust you in other words. But you didn't, did you? And you started to withdraw——'

'Dominic,' she broke in urgently, 'it wasn't a lack of *trust*——'

He said through his teeth, 'What was it, then?'

She drew a shaky breath. 'I knew... I always knew that you couldn't stay spiritually handicapped as you thought you were. I *always* recognised the possibility that some day the... right one would come along for you. Jenny—I couldn't *help* thinking—once I knew how she felt about you, that what you needed was sort of embodied in Jenny. Such a lovely mix of innocence and wisdom and certainly not the muddled mess I am,' she said starkly.

'If that isn't a lack of trust I don't know what is,' he said harshly, 'but go on. So you appointed yourself keeper of my soul. Did you decide you loved me too much to keep me chained to your side? Would you even have gone so far as to hand me to her on a platter, I wonder?' he said with bitter contempt. 'What if I won't go?'

'Because of guilt?' she whispered. 'That will help none of us.'

'No, damn it!' He strode over to her chair and hauled her up out of it brutally. 'Because I am chained to you whether you like it or not. Do you think I would have flown to Singapore and then straight home because I suddenly knew that, without me, anything could happen, you could talk yourself into anything—do you think I'd have done that if there weren't a link so strong between us it can't be severed? Not by me... Do you think—you once told me about the heights and the depths—

don't you think the depths I've sunk to since I got home mean something?'

'Dominic...' She winced as he shook her then with equally savagery pulled her into his arms.

'Are you going to hold the rubbish I spouted on Hayman against me for the rest of my life? Despite the last, loving months when I've tried to *show* you? Don't you know that I held back from making love to you after Nicky was born because I couldn't help linking it with the pain and suffering you went through? What *would* make you believe in me, Stephanie?'

Despite being in his arms and feeling the thud of his heart against her breasts, she was frightened, she realised. Not of him, at last, but of whether she could ever make him understand that he'd banished her fears for once and for all.

'Dominic, if you're trying to tell me you love me——'

'I'm trying to tell you that the thought of you not really believing in me and my love is driving me crazy and to think that you could walk away from me——'

She put up a shaky hand and touched his cheek, where she'd hit it. 'I *wasn't*. I was only going to spend a few days with Nan—but yes, because I was miserable and wretched and—all the things you accused me of. And yes, again, because I lacked faith then. I did—at first I didn't say anything about Jenny in the spirit of what *you* said. I thought it was better left unsaid but after Melissa... perhaps being in a postnatal condition didn't help and perhaps...' she stared up at him with a dawning of something in her eyes that was both heartbroken and hopeful '...you'd better not embrace any more pretty girls at airports when I'm like that. Oh, God, how could I have been such a fool? But you see you never *told* me and sometimes you showed me...that I was only important to you for one reason. So, I still thought it was only me.'

'Only you in love?' At last his voice softened.

'Oh, yes,' she whispered. 'In love—the only thing that's ever changed is that now I'm also totally dependent on you and I can't ever pretend to myself again that the thought of living without you isn't like dying.' She smiled tremulously then began to cry.

He held her so hard that for a time it was difficult to breathe then he picked her up and took her over to the settee and kissed away the tears. 'Don't for one minute imagine I'm feeling as self-righteous as I may have sounded,' he said huskily at last as he slipped his hands beneath her jumper to warm them on her breasts. 'If anyone had told me what the depths were really like I wouldn't have believed them. That in my desperation I would want to do anything to bind you to me, even hurt you— it came as quite a shock but I still couldn't help myself.' He held her close again suddenly and she could feel the intensity of his guilt.

'Don't,' she said very gently.

'I must tell you all of it, though,' he said unsteadily and lifted his head. 'You were right about someone breaking the spiritual drought but all the time it was *you*. Why I couldn't have admitted it to myself, to us both, I'll never understand. Why it took the thought of losing you to really open up the depths and heights will always be a mystery. Can you ever forgive—that?'

'Oh, Dominic,' she said softly, 'if you think I haven't been without understanding and humility and not very wise sometimes, often, you must have a short memory.'

He kissed her deeply. 'By the way,' he said, his mouth still lingering on her skin, 'the only embracing I did at the airport was in a supremely avuncular manner that was calculated to kill any girl's dreams stone dead.'

'You don't have to—I know now.' She kissed his wrist. 'Nor do you have to worry about making love to me; it won't ever be as bad as that again, but anyway I'd willingly go through it once more to prove my love and faith.'

'Stephanie...' he buried his face in her hair then looked into her eyes and said with an unsteady smile '...I think I'm a little drunk.'

Her eyes widened.

'Drunk on the perfume of your skin which is like no other, the feel of you, the thought of your body opening to mine. Is,' he said wryly, 'there any chance of this peace lasting?'

She opened her mouth but right on cue, perhaps sensing that he was about to be relegated from his parents' minds, Nicholas Rayburn intervened.

'No,' she said with a soft, tremulous smile, 'but later...'

*   *   *

Later, Dominic said, as they lay side by side holding hands, 'Stay here. I'm going to make us something to eat.'

'I can——'

'No, you can't,' he said dictatorially and leant up on his elbow and pushed his dark hair out of his eyes. 'For the next couple of days there are only two things you need to concentrate on. I'll do the rest.'

'Two?'

'Yes, two,' he agreed gravely but his eyes glinted wickedly. 'Care to speculate?'

'Nicky?' she hazarded.

'Of course.'

Her lips curved and she slid her hands up his chest and her eyes were serene and loving. 'And . . . you?'

He caught his breath. 'How did you guess?'

'It must have been what I had in mind—I love you,' she whispered and was not allowed to speak further for quite a few minutes.

Later again in the evening, when Nicky was asleep in her arms, ready to be put to bed for the night, she looked up and saw Dominic watching them from across the firelit room, standing tall and still in the doorway. It struck her suddenly, bringing tears to her eyes, that her dark captor was now her lover and protector, her husband in every sense of the word at last. And that their communication was now so perfect that it needed no words for him to understand her thoughts—the way he crossed to her side and stroked her hair as she leant her head against him said it all.

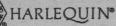
HARLEQUIN®

PRESENTS *plus*

Meet Lewis Marsh, the man who walked out of Lacey's
life twenty years ago. Now he's back, but is time really a
cure for love?

And then there's widower Jim Proctor, whose young
daughter, Maude, needs a mother. Lucy needs a job,
but does she really need a husband?

These are just some of the passionate men and women
you'll discover each month in Harlequin Presents
Plus—two longer and dramatic new romances by some
of the best-loved authors writing for Harlequin
Presents. Share their exciting stories—their heartaches
and triumphs—as each falls in love.

Don't miss
A CURE FOR LOVE by Penny Jordan,
Harlequin Presents Plus #1575
and
THE WIDOW'S MITE by Emma Goldrick,
Harlequin Presents Plus #1576

Harlequin Presents Plus
The best has just gotten better!

Available in August wherever Harlequin books are sold.

Relive the romance...
Harlequin and Silhouette
are proud to present

A program of collections of three complete novels by the most
requested authors with the most requested themes. Be sure to
look for one volume each month with three complete novels by
top name authors.

In June: **NINE MONTHS** Penny Jordan
                           Stella Cameron
                           Janice Kaiser

**Three women pregnant and alone. But a lot can
happen in nine months!**

In July: **DADDY'S**   Kristin James
          HOME   Naomi Horton
                           Mary Lynn Baxter

**Daddy's Home... and his presence is long
overdue!**

In August: **FORGOTTEN**   Barbara Kaye
           PAST   Pamela Browning
                           Nancy Martin

**Do you dare to create a future if you've forgotten
the past?**

Available at your favorite retail outlet.

REQ-G

**WHEN STOLEN MOMENTS
ARE ALL YOU HAVE...**

The sun is hot and you've got a few minutes
to catch some rays....

And what better way to spend the time than with
SUMMER MADNESS—our summer promotion that features
six new individual short contemporary stories.

SIZZLE	Jennifer Crusie
ANNIVERSARY WALTZ	Anne Marie Duquette
MAGGIE AND HER COLONEL	Merline Lovelace
PRAIRIE SUMMER	Alina Roberts
THE SUGAR CUP	Annie Sims
LOVE ME NOT	Barbara Stewart

Each story is a complete romance that's just the perfect length
for the busy woman of the nineties . . . but still providing the
perfect blend of adventure, sensuality and, of course, romance!

Look for the special displays in July and share some of the
Summer Madness!

HSM-1

 **W❁RLDWIDE LIBRARY**

THREE UNFORGETTABLE HEROINES
THREE AWARD-WINNING AUTHORS

MAVERICK HEARTS

A unique collection of historical short stories that
capture the spirit of America's last frontier.

HEATHER GRAHAM POZZESSERE—over 10 million copies
of her books in print worldwide
Lonesome Rider—The story of an Eastern widow and the
renegade half-breed who becomes her protector.

PATRICIA POTTER—an author whose books are consistently
Waldenbooks bestsellers
Against the Wind—Two people, battered by heartache, prove
that love can heal all.

JOAN JOHNSTON—award-winning Western historical author
with 17 books to her credit
One Simple Wish—A woman with a past discovers that
dreams really do come true.

Join us for an exciting journey West with
UNTAMED
Available in July, wherever Harlequin books are sold.

MAV93

Discover the glorious triumph of three
extraordinary couples fueled by a powerful
passion to defy the past in

Lingering Shadows

The dramatic story of six fascinating men and
women who find the strength to step out of the
shadows and into the light of a passionate future.

Linked by relentless ambition and by desire, each
must confront private demons in a riveting struggle
for power. Together they must find the strength to
emerge from the lingering shadows of the past, into
the dawning promise of the future.

Look for this powerful new blockbuster by *New
York Times* bestselling author

PENNY JORDAN

Available in August at your favorite retail outlet.

PJLS93